ARCHITECT OF FATE

F. Sharon Swope
&
Genilee Swope Parente

Architect of Fate

GSP Publishing

©2017

An e-book edition of this book was published in 2017 by GSP Publishing.

For information contact:
GSP Publishing
4228 Ashmere Circle
Dumfries, VA 22025
swopeparente@gmail.com

Cover design by Harshani Fernando

Author photo by Aleda Johnson Powell

ISBN 978-0-9995036-0-7

ACKNOWLEDGEMENTS

ARCHITECT OF FATE took more time than any other book in the Fate series. That's because, as you'll soon discover, the plot we created is complicated and brings back many of the characters we've met along the way. We have perfected our craft as we go, and we've been delighted with each step, including this new phase of the story. We've also received a lot of guidance and help on our journey.

We believe the reason you write is so that others will read. That's why our first acknowledgement goes out to the fans that have come to our signings and book events to let us know that, like us, they've fallen a little more in love with Sam Osborne and The Fate Series with each book. Doing what you love is often not an easy task, and we could not have continued down the difficult path of pursuing our passion if our readers had not stopped by or written to tell us how much they enjoy our books and look forward to what comes next.

We'd like to thank our editor Tam Albright for sticking with us through the transition from a traditional publishing house to independent publishing. We acknowledge how much her talents have improved our books.

We'd also like to thank some old friends who returned to give us more expertise. Elvis Bello provided us insight so that we could place one of our heroes as a Richmond police officer. We know we probably don't have all the procedures down correctly, but we needed his law enforcement background to get started. The FBI's Investigative Publicity and Public Affairs Unit helped us set up our "task force" with Richmond as the lead. We asked and got expert advice from

Jane and Rick Jacobs, whose background in pharmacology enabled us to keep one of our "victims" alive. Johanna Muench continues to astonish us with the insight she provides on our plots. Finally, thanks to Mark Swope for serving as mom's Internet research machine and one of our beta readers.

With this book, we also sought help from new areas. Long-time supporter Joe D'Agostino read the initial draft and gave us not only his encouragement, but his thoughts on this particular story. Lourie Reichenberg provided insight on the psychology of one of our characters.

We want to thank the regional office of Applebee's, Potomac Family Dining, for helping us throw a terrific bash in celebration of our last book, *Treasured Fate*. It's the second time your hospitality has helped us launch one of our books, and it was just as fun as the first.

Finally, we never would have begun this journey if not for the encouragement of children's book author Allyn M. Stotz. She's gone through so many of our ups and downs with us, but continues to plow forward with her own creative efforts, which provide an inspiration for us. You're not only a talented writer, Allyn, you're also our muse.

TABLE OF CONTENTS

PROLOGUE

WHY OH WHY won't that man stop screaming?

I can't move my arms; I can't see anything. Am I dead?

If I'm dead, I'm not in Heaven. No one in Heaven would allow that man to scream so loudly. Please shut him up.

Heaven wouldn't have sirens and trucks and shouting. They wouldn't have people crying. Why are people crying?

I must be in Hell. I did something terrible, now I'm in hell. Did I do something to the man. Is that why he's screaming?

Can't someone shut him up?

I want to open my eyes, but I'm afraid. I want to stop his screaming, but I don't know how. I want to ask someone to help me. But I can't talk, and I wish I couldn't hear. I wish I wasn't so horribly afraid.

I try to move, but my body won't budge. I try to lift my legs, but someone is holding them down. I think someone is sitting on my legs.

"Freddie, hurry with that shot."

Ohmygod. They're going to shoot me. Why would someone shoot me? Why don't they shoot the man who won't stop screaming and put him out of his misery?

What a terrible thing to say. I'm a terrible person, and I'm in Hell, and now they're going to shoot me.

Someone's trying to pick me up. Where are they taking me to shoot me? I want to fight them; I have no muscles or bones or strength. I'm on a board on my back and people's arms and hands are all over me, holding me down, touching me when I don't want to be touched. I should open my eyes, see who it is. But I don't want to. I don't want to feel the horror that is out there.

I don't want to see the man screaming.

They're lifting my board up, putting me into something. Is it a coffin? Why are they putting me in my coffin if I'm already dead?

I don't care. I really don't care. My muscles are turning to water. My thoughts are drifting away, and I don't want them back. I welcome the darkness that surrounds me. I want the blackness that approaches.

If only someone would shut the man up so I could sleep.

"Marjorie! Help me! Make it go away! Make this all go away! Where's my boy? Where's my girls?

"Marjorie. Come back Marjorie. Please, please don't leave me here in Hell."

CHAPTER ONE

HOW COULD SHE LEAVE this mess behind? Mark Brady thought.

He stared at the mountain of papers he'd released from a hat box in his mom's closet. He hated being here in the house, going through all her stuff. But he and his two siblings agreed it had to be done. They wouldn't be selling the house for a while, but they needed to start sorting through the life of the woman they'd loved so much and lost.

He and Janet had come all the way from Richmond to start the process two weeks after the funeral. Bill lived closer and agreed to help when the time came to sell.

Mark had volunteered to tackle the paperwork not just because he was the most organized, but because he needed to find his birth certificate. He'd been accepted into a special law enforcement training program in the U.K., his first time out of the country.

He needed the original certificate to get a passport and enroll in the program.

His mom told all of them she kept important papers in the boxes on this shelf; but he couldn't believe she'd tossed them together without any effort to put them in order. It just didn't fit with the way they were raised.

Her words echoed in his brain.

"Your socks do not belong outside your closet door. Your schoolbag does not belong on your bed. Everything has its place, and if you keep that in mind, you'll always be able to find what you need."

Mark sighed deeply and ran one hand through his dark brown hair.

"I guess the papers had their place all right—all together in a couple of boxes."

He rubbed his face with both palms. He supposed this fatigue was one of the stages of grief he'd read about. He'd gone through denial briefly when he'd learned of her sudden heart attack. None of the kids had known she had heart troubles. They'd just celebrated her sixtieth a few years ago. How could she be gone?

After he'd finally stopped denying, he went to the next stage: Anger. Why hadn't she been taking care of herself? What's more, why hadn't he realized or his siblings known she was neglecting her health? She'd been seeing a heart specialist only a short time and hadn't told her children how serious it was. They could have encouraged her to get on a health kick. They could have visited more often.

Mark sighed and continued sorting. *She hadn't wanted to worry them of course.* It was just like their Ma to take on the burden of her own bad news so her children could go on with their busy lives.

Was he now in the bargaining phase? *Maybe if we can clean up her affairs, the pain will lessen.*

It wasn't working.

Instead, he remained angry and felt like he was slipping into guilt and depression. What was the use of all this sorting? She wasn't coming back.

What will we all do without her?

Mom had been the base of their family—the steady rock in every storm. She supported the long hours their father had put into his career as an accountant. She fought the battles with contractors when service to her family was subpar, carted the kids to the emergency room, talked to teachers on their behalf, encouraged them to pursue their dreams.

When she'd been widowed six years ago, she'd worked through her own grief mostly in private, giving her children the comfort they needed instead of licking her own wounds. He and his siblings had just taken for granted she'd be there forever to guide them—to help them get through every major crisis and phase of life.

She couldn't help them with this one, however, and she wouldn't be around to see if Mark ever got married or had his own kids. He was glad she'd witnessed his career success—a law enforcement degree, a master's program, his first few positions. She'd been delighted when he finally made detective in Richmond.

But what had all that cost in terms of his relationship with her?

He'd always promised himself that once he got through school, once he got his first real job, once he made detective, he'd be back here to Michigan more often for visits. Now that wasn't going to happen.

Instead, he was left with a pile of papers that meant nothing. Bills marked 'paid'; receipts from Green Thumb gardening, Marshall Home Goods, and Gourmet Cookware; bank statements from dozens of years of trying to keep within the household budget; auto repair estimates and statements for work done years ago, all seemingly tossed into boxes.

He rose from his perch on the bed to stretch his back. He was tired of going through her belongings; he was tired of the ache of missing her, and this wasn't making anything better.

Janet's head appeared through the open door. "Making any progress?"

Mark shook his head. "This is one hell of a wreck pile—can you believe it? We don't even know how many death certificates we need for insurance and other things, and where we'll need to send them until we sort things out a little and find the right doc-umentation. And I can't find my original birth certif-icate."

Janet walked up to him and gently laid a hand on his shoulder. Just gazing into her warm brown eyes brought him comfort. He'd always loved her down-home clean look, her eager grin, her shiny brown hair, her strong hands. Just like with Ma, she was an anchor in his life.

"Why don't you go help Bill in the garage, and I'll take over here. He's boxing up Dad's tools. Six years since he died, but I swear, Mom never threw a thing of his away."

Mark reached out and patted her cheek. He was pretty sure he'd already found anything he was going to find in these boxes, but it felt good to let his sister take over: she was already assuming the role of the family's matriarch.

"A second pair of eyes is good, Sis. And maybe she had another place for important papers. I laid aside a couple of insurance forms and bank state-ments we'll need."

He rose and left to walk down the hall, pausing long enough to study a few family portraits. In the largest and latest one, the girls sat stiff-backed on chairs. The boys stood behind the girls, his father's hand on his mother's shoulder. It was taken his junior year of high school. The boys and Dad wore the ties and coats they so hated; Janet and his mom were dressed in matching dresses that didn't seem to fit either the mother's forty-plus age or the girl's ten-year old scrawny frame. Mark stood behind Janet's chair, his five-foot-eight, solid frame a contrast to the tall thin build of his brother and father.

His eyes traveled to an earlier picture on the wall. Mom and Dad looked so young, but he'd always loved the enthusiasm and joy that emanated from this image. Dad clutched the hand of both the toddler Bill and Bill's "big" brother Mark, who actually wasn't much bigger than Bill, despite the fact he was two years older. Mom held the newborn Janet on her lap, a glow on her face.

They must have been ecstatic to finally have a baby girl, Mark thought. The house contained dozens of baby shots of Janet, a few of Bill, and none of Mark that were still on display.

He continued down the hall. Maybe some of the important family papers were kept in Dad's den. He sat at the desk, gazing around and remembering how driven his father had been. Mark may not have inherited his dad's looks, but he'd inherited the drive.

He had always loved pushing himself—in school, on the field, competing with others. He'd been cracking the books or sweating away on the soccer field, while his buddies drank themselves sick and chased skin in halter tops.

He rifled through desk drawers, but found nothing. It shouldn't have surprised him: Mom was the one who gathered and kept things. Dad's den was neat as a pin: books on the shelves, papers long gone or, more likely, handed off to Mom.

They'd all handed off stuff to Mom, who, just like with the toys and books, dumped them together in the right "bin." If he'd paid less attention to his ambitions and more attention to what she was doing, maybe he could have helped her sort out her life.

CHAPTER TWO

Richmond, VA

THE TWO COLLEGE GIRLS sipped from cardboard cups with plastic lids. They sat at an outside table despite the lingering cool of the fall, neither aware of the man standing on the other side of a hedge.

The young women had been at the coffee shop for over twenty minutes—most of that time had been inside among the crowds of people, but they must have sought the solace of the outside, where the weather meant no other tables were occupied. The man had strolled casually out the door a few moments after they did, glancing their way as he passed. They hadn't seen him. The girl with the blonde hair was on the verge of crying. The one with the curly red hair stroked the back of the blonde's hand, attempting to soothe her friend.

He'd found this spot on a nearby cement planter behind a thick wall of bushes that mostly hid him from their view. By leaning back and peering through the bushes, he could see them. They were paying no attention, and he could just make out what they said.

"I know it's a shock, but you know he loved you. What does it matter what the circumstances were?" the redhead said.

"You're right of course. I know you're right. It doesn't change my feelings about him. I just have to know the truth," her friend replied.

"I guess I understand that." The red curls were bouncing up and down. "But Carla, I don't think this is a good idea."

"You're probably right about that as well." The blonde picked up a lock of her long silky hair and began to play with the ends.

The redhead leaned back in her chair and tilted her face up to the sun as if the warmth of its rays could help her absorb her friend's problems. After a few moments of quiet, she stood.

"I'm sorry. I gotta go. I'm late for class as it is. Can we talk about this some more later?"

The blonde didn't move. She continued stroking the piece of hair studying each strand closely.

"Carla?" the redhead said.

The blonde looked up, just now noticing her friend was on her feet.

"Of course you're right about all this. Look, we can talk about this tonight? Or tomorrow. It's … whatever. 'k?" The words came out in a jumble as she stood and picked up the small pile of books still on the table. A piece of paper fluttered to the ground and she stooped to pick it up, placing it inside one of the books. She smiled at the redhead and gave her a one-armed hug. The friends turned in the opposite directions and walked off.

Good girl, darling, the man thought. *You took the note with you. See you soon, my love.*

CHAPTER THREE

Wednesday, November 2

MARK HAD BEEN FLIPPING through scrapbooks and albums for over an hour when Bill popped his head into the open doorway, startling his brother.

"What's up?" Bill asked. "Don't you ever sleep?"

"I could say the same about you," Mark told him. "It's two a.m. Aren't you finished with that garage yet? You've been chipping away at it for two days."

"Nah. I mean, Dad had organized drawers for his tools, but that garage is *completely* packed with other stuff. I guess Mom didn't feel like she could part with any of it. Or maybe she didn't want to do what we're doing now. Any luck finding the birth certificate?"

Mark shook his head. "I thought maybe she put some of her papers in one of these." He swept his hand at the coffee table, where scrapbooks and photo books lay open.

Mark held up the album he was currently studying—a worn leather tome that dated back before the Brady children had come into the picture.

"I keep getting caught up in the past, flipping through the pages," Mark said. "I don't know this photo album, though."

The book came back to his lap, and Bill plopped down beside him, taking half the heavy album onto his lap.

The old sofa emitted a soft sigh. As far back as the boys could remember, it had always been part of this room, a room they had nicknamed, "the really living" room. It got its name because the house had a formal room for greeting guests, a family room for daily activities and school studies, and this room: an eclectic mix of sewing scraps, games and puzzles, and miscellaneous storage. It was where their mom always said she could contain their mess and where she'd allow them to get as loud as they wanted.

"As nice as Ma kept the rest of this house, I believe this was always my favorite place," Bill said. He glanced around at the neatly labeled bins where Mom required them to stow whatever toy or game or distraction they had before leaving the room.

Mark nodded, mentally reading off the labels on the bins: "school art," "picture books," "readers," "photo albums."

"And yet you can see that even here, she had a problem with actually throwing any of this stuff out," he said. "I mean, we haven't read picture books in twenty-something years. She just couldn't stand to get rid of her favorite stories."

Bill grinned his crooked grin and returned his concentration to the heavy book on their laps.

Mark loved that crooked smile almost as much as he loved Janet's warmth. It was so reflective of his relaxed brother—carefree and easily amused. Why couldn't he have absorbed some of his brother's attitude towards life?

Mark studied his brother's face.

"You look so much like Dad. Really, almost from the time you were a baby. That same aristocratic snotty nose," he teased.

Bill flicked Mark on the arm, then turned back to the album to point out a picture. "I see that beautifully sculpted nose on this guy standing next to Mom, too. Who do you suppose *that* is?"

Bill tapped the picture with his finger.

"You suppose it was a cousin of Dad's?" he asked.

The tall, thin, handsome man stood with one arm around their mother. Dad was in the picture, but unlike the others, he was not smiling and his forehead was creased. His lips were turned down slightly.

"If that was Dad's cousin, it appears he didn't like the guy much," Mark said.

Janet's arrival interrupted the conversation. "What on earth are you two doing?" she asked between yawns. "It's the middle of the night. You're both supposed to be snoring."

Bill patted the seat beside him. "We're too tired and wound up to sleep, but you're just in time. Who's this man with his arm around Ma? He seems awfully chummy and Dad's not too happy."

Janet walked over and settled down beside her brothers. She squinted at the picture. "I think that must be Uncle Gerald—Dad's skeleton in the closet," she said.

"*Skeleton?*" the brothers said in unison, turning to gape at Janet. "How come we never heard of him?" Mark added.

"Mom and Dad didn't talk about him. Probably because he's always been a few steps away from going back to jail," Janet said.

Bill and Mark gazed wide-eyed at their sister, who had uttered this news with complete calm.

"We really had a jailbird in the family?" Bill asked. "How come you know this and we don't? Did we ever meet him?"

Janet sat back on the couch and sighed. Mark saw the blue circles of exhaustion around her eyes and felt his gut twist in guilt. Both he and Bill had let their baby sister deal with Mom's last years while they led their busy lives. Of course Janet knew more than they did. Mom probably had one-on-one chats with her daughter during Janet's frequent visits to Michigan.

"We met him only once that I know of—and I think we were pretty young. I don't remember, but you might, Mark. Mom told me our uncle had come for a visit, but Dad came home and kicked him out."

Mark had no recollection of the visit.

"Did Mom keep in touch with him then?" he asked.

"Yes, I think she felt really bad that Dad didn't get along with his own sibling. She had an email for him and occasionally wrote. She mentioned him not too long ago."

"How come she never said anything to us?" Bill asked.

Janet's second yawn was expansive. She rubbed her tired eyes.

"I don't think Dad wanted us associated with him. Mom just told me about it this past year. He apparently served time for forgery. He made a ton of money before he got caught—he even tried to send her some of that money in the early days. She sent it right back because she knew it would make Dad mad. But she kept tabs on him, I guess just because he was family."

Bill grinned and poked Mark in the ribs. "There's your solution to the birth certificate, brother," he said. "Get ahold of Uncle Gerald and ask him to make you a new one!"

Mark tossed a fake glare Bill's way, then laughed.

"I'm sure that would go over well with my new captain," he said.

CHAPTER FOUR

Wednesday, November 9

ONE WEEK LATER, Mark was back in Richmond facing that captain: his new boss Robert McCoy. The three Brady children had agreed to return to Traverse City a last time at the end of this month. If he didn't find the document he needed then, he'd get a replacement—he didn't need it until next summer. Right now, he needed to be here, anxious to get into the new job. He'd only been in this position two months, and his boss was assigning him to lead his first case.

Mark set a cardboard coffee container on his boss's desk, then reached his hand toward a file his boss was offering him.

Bob handed the paperwork over and picked up the Starbucks container, savoring his first long sip.

"If you're seeking brownie points, you've made your first score," he said.

Putting the cup down, he leaned forward to rest his forearms on his desk.

"I know I haven't had time to prep you, but there's a young woman in your office this morning who can explain what's in that file. Her name is Melissa Burns, and she filed an official police report yesterday morning on a young woman who's gone missing. We did some preliminary follow up while you were on your way back here: called the university, the roommate's friends, her family. But we haven't been able to locate the missing girl, and it's time to go deeper into this."

Mark rose from his chair, already studying what was in the file. Without taking his eyes off what he was reading, he nodded to his boss and left his office, then flipped through the report on his way. He read enough to absorb that the missing person was a college student named Carla Dunlap and that Melissa Burns was her roommate. When he arrived at his office door, he saw the young woman, her back to the door, running her hands through an abundance of short red curls on her head.

Mark stood in the threshold and cleared his throat to announce his presence. She jumped slightly and turned to face him, and what he saw in her dark blue eyes struck home: the woman was deeply afraid. The puffiness around her eyes indicated she'd spent some time crying and before he'd even asked a question, he felt a tug at his heart. Something about the petite redhead made him want to go to her, lay a hand on her shoulder and promise he'd help her in any way he could.

Mark mentally shook himself, walked to his desk and sat, putting the file in front of him on the desk. He opened the file and took out the top sheet, studying it for a moment before looking up, only to be drawn back into those eyes.

"Your roommate is missing."

His comment opened the floodgates.

"Yes. Oh god. She's been gone for almost two days. I know something's wrong. I feel it." She put both hands on his desk trying to steady herself.

"She's not one to run off. She's not one to get drunk and stay somewhere, and even if she did, I know she'd call me."

Her hands left the desktop and landed in her lap. She slumped backwards in her chair and sighed. *How many hours had she already spent worrying,* Mark wondered.

"Why don't we start from the beginning," Mark said. "Tell me what happened Monday."

She took another breath, letting it out slowly.

"We're both grad students at the University of Richmond. We live in an apartment not far from cam-·pus. On Monday, we left about the same time— around eleven I think. She had a computer class. I was on my way to Psych 404—I'm a psych major. We agreed to meet for a late lunch and a trip to the bookstore after our classes."

Melissa studied her palms as though they held the facts that could help her figure out what hap-pened.

"And she didn't show?" Mark asked.

Her head came up and her eyes trapped him again.

"She didn't show. She didn't call. And she didn't answer her cell phone. I knew right away something was off. I know that sounds crazy but …"

"You called her friends." Mark said, looking down at the paperwork.

"She doesn't have that many, but I checked with those I knew who lived on campus or nearby. I called campus police to see if anything had happened at the college, then called the local hospital to make sure there hadn't been a car accident or something. I didn't call the Richmond police until late that night, and they told me how to file a report."

Her eyes started to fill and Mark instinctively reached for a tissue and handed it over.

"I should have gone in that night to file. But I listened to the people who said she'd probably skipped out on class to party with friends or maybe took off somewhere because she was sick of school. Now its Wednesday and she's not home and hasn't called or even texted."

Melissa put the tissue to one eye trying to absorb the tears before they could spill over. It seemed to work.

Mark could have told her how often skipping out on life occurred, but he kept quiet. She didn't need his attempts at reasoning after already hearing the same thing from others.

"I get that other students may have done that in the past. I get that it's standard for the police to encourage you not to panic at first," Melissa continued, seemingly reading his thoughts. His eyes came up to see her studying him. Was she using her psychology skills to figure *him* out? She glanced at his badge.

"This is Carla, Detective Brady. She and I have become really close. She tells me everything. She wouldn't just run away without telling me."

Mark nodded his head once then looked back down at the report.

"It says here you notified her mom late Monday night?"

His eyes came back up to see despair cross her features. She put both palms on her cheeks and rubbed, as if trying to erase what she was feeling.

"I didn't want to call her, but I was desperate. I thought maybe she'd gone home. I know I worried Mrs. Dunlap, but what could I do? I had to know where she was."

She dropped her hands back into her lap.

"Carla told me recently that her mom is going through a difficult time—she lost her husband last year and it's close to the anniversary of his death. I thought maybe Carla decided her mother needed support and went home suddenly."

The tears came back, and Melissa couldn't stop them this time.

"Now I've scared her poor mom to death, and I still have no answers."

Mark offered her another tissue and returned to the report. He didn't like how this crying girl was tugging at his heart. His training had taught him he needed to remain detached to keep his brain functioning in investigative mode.

Yet Mark also recalled the words of Professor Bellow, his mentor. *Empathy, not sympathy, makes for the best cops.*

He wasn't sure why this woman elicited a response, but it didn't matter right now. He had some digging to do, and he didn't know exactly why, but he believed her fear was real.

God, I hope for her sake my first investigation doesn't turn out to be a murder.

CHAPTER FIVE

MARK FILLED UP three pages of notes as Melissa explained how she and Carla had become friends their freshman year after being placed together in a dorm room.

"You have to understand how excited I was to have a roomy. I've never had a sibling, much less a sister," she said. Mark could see the tightness around her eyes and lips relax slightly as she left the uncertainty of the present to visit the past.

"I loved leaving the small town where I grew up to come to the big city of Richmond and the big college of Richmond U. I was pursuing my dream: studying the complexities of the human brain, and I'd been texting the girl the university assigned as my roommate the entire summer before college began. I couldn't wait to meet her!"

She leaned back in her chair, an almost-smile breaking through.

"Anyway, I showed up on our first day, full of excitement and expectation. I walk into our new room, and I'm greeted by dozens of teddy bears dressed in an assortment of girly clothes mostly in pink and purple. I thought: 'Ohmygod. I'm stuck with a crack pot!'"

She tried to laugh, but it came out sounding like a cough, and she covered her mouth, either trying to expunge the humor or maybe trying to hold it in place a little longer. Mark was just glad to catch his first glimpse of a lighter Melissa Burns—a pleasant memory had broken through the worry about the present.

"Then she walks in and instead of the geeky immature girl I'd imagined would have a room full of stuffed animals, she's striking … blonde and tall with exquisite features … everything I'm not. She's also friendly and chatty and full of life, not apologizing for the bears or even explaining them. I was swept up in her enthusiasm."

Mark guessed the "everything I'm not," referred to the height difference and coloring, because he personally thought the woman sitting across from him was striking in her own pretty, perky way.

"Anyway, maybe because we *are* so different, we seemed to really hit it off and quickly became best friends," she said.

She captured his eyes again.

"And we've stayed that way. I'm telling you—something is wrong here."

After the words were in the air, her gaze dropped to her lap like she didn't want to continue.

Where did her thoughts suddenly travel? Mark wondered.

Melissa left after an hour of talking. Mark made an appointment to come by their apartment the next day if no one heard from Carla. Now he sat staring at his notes and making a list of where to go with this investigation:

- Background checks on Carla, Melissa, the friends Melissa mentioned.
- Search the apartment for clues.
- Interview neighbors.
- Talk to the mother.
- Talk to the friends in this area, including any of Carla's boyfriends.

It was all standard stuff seeking information Carla's roommate didn't know or wouldn't talk about.

Mark visualized the freckled face, the red curls and the way Melissa had poured out her heart. As open as she had been with her thoughts—as comfortable talking about her relationship with her roommate, her own background and what she knew about Carla, Mark couldn't help feeling like the redhead was holding something back.

Thursday, Nov. 10
Melissa's and Carla's apartment was sparsely furnished, but tidy and filled with inexpensive keepsakes. Mark knew immediately which of the

bedrooms was Carla's because most surfaces had at least one teddy bear. As Melissa had described, they all had dresses or tutus and cute bows or ribbons on their heads. A few even had flowing locks of hair.

Wonder if the woman has a season pass to Build-a-Bear? Mark thought.

Donning a pair of rubber gloves, he picked up a few of the bears and put them back down, then turned to the desk. With permission from Melissa, he went through the few pieces of mail, finding nothing. He turned on the laptop perched on the desk and did a cursory search, explaining as he went that he'd take the computer in to be examined by his department's technical team. Then he began a thorough search of every closet and drawer.

He didn't come up with anything worthwhile until he spotted a crumpled piece of paper underneath the desk. He picked it up, smoothed it out and read: "Dad, eleven-thirty, McDonalds."

"Dad?" Mark looked over to Melissa. "Didn't you tell me her father died last year?"

Melissa got up from her perch on the bed and went over to gaze at the paper, which Mark had slipped into a plastic bag. "I don't understand it," she said softly.

"Am I reading the word wrong?" he asked. "The handwriting is scribbly and small."

She studied it for a minute more, squinting at the tiny handwriting, then got up and rifled through a desk drawer. Pulling out a magnifying glass, she peered at the paper. Finally, she shook her head and said, "Her handwriting is sometimes atrocious. But I'm pretty sure this says 'Dad.' How can this be—unless…"

"Unless?"

Melissa's eyes rounded, and Mark saw the moment she decided it was better to tell what she knew.

"Unless she found her real father."

Mark reached out slowly and took the note back from Melissa. He tried to keep his voice even as he asked: "Her *real* father?"

Two bright spots of color appeared on her cheeks, competing with her freckles.

"She…she told me just recently there was some question on who her father was. That it might not be Charles Dunlap."

"Why didn't you tell me this at our first meeting?"

Melissa's eyes narrowed, and Mark sensed a fence going up—a fence designed to protect Carla.

"I'm not one to betray a confidence, and she made me promise to keep it to myself. She'd just learned about it herself a few weeks ago. She overheard her mother and aunt talking about the possibility that Mr. Dunlap might not be her father. It was a private conversation she wasn't supposed to hear, and she shared it with me only because it upset her."

But you didn't think this was significant? Mark thought. He didn't want to run up against that defensive fence, however. So he said nothing. Just nodded his head once. He'd let her realize her mistake at her own pace.

"It can't have anything to do with this. It can't," Melissa said. But the anger was gone, replaced by a question. "Can it?"

"I don't know," Mark said. "But this is significant. Our best hope for finding out something is to check out everything that's happened recently and everyone from her background. Thank you for telling me." He got his notebook out of his back pocket and made a notation, then slipped the note beneath one of the pages.

Mark went next to the neighbors' apartments. No one seemed to have much information about Carla, which wasn't a surprise since Melissa explained that neither grad student had much time to get to know others in the building. No one mentioned seeing her with a man or a possible boyfriend or much of anyone except Melissa.

Mark finally hit pay dirt in the form of Todd Walker, a guy from apartment two-B across the hall. Todd reported seeing Carla the morning of the disappearance.

"It was noon, and I was home sick that day," the tall, thirty-year-old man with slightly greasy hair, reported. Todd had lived in the building for just a few weeks; he'd taken the apartment because he worked on the University of Richmond campus as an accountant in the administrative offices. He knew Carla because she was a student—he'd seen her on campus and walking home, and had a few conversations in the hallway.

"Noon? Are you sure about that?" Mark asked referring to the notation he'd just made. The timing contradicted what Melissa had said about the two of them attending individual classes then meeting up for a late lunch. Carla had either skipped her eleven o'clock or been let out early. She and Melissa weren't due to meet up until one-thirty. Why had Carla come home? And why leave the house so early? Their designated meeting spot was only a fifteen-minute walk away.

"Positive," Todd said. "That's when 'Days of Our Lives' starts and I heard her at her door, fumbling with keys."

Mark looked up from his notebook to study his interviewee. The guy was squirrelly, running his fingertips alongside both sides of his mouth as if he were nervous. But he didn't evade Mark's eyes.

"You can hear her from across the hall?" Mark asked.

"Well … I was going by on my way to the kitchen. When I heard someone outside my door, I glanced out my peephole."

"So that's when you saw her. Did she seem upset or in a hurry? Was she with anyone?"

"Nope. She was all alone. She had her coat off and slung over her arm already and wore a really nice sweater …"

"Can you describe the sweater?" Mark prodded.

"Pink. With flowers and a lot of fuzz," Todd said. His words collaborated with what Melissa had said she'd been wearing that day.

"And some really tight jeans," Todd added.

The guy obviously did more than "glance," Mark thought.

"But she was alone," he asked. "Was she carrying anything?"

"Just her backpack, which, come to think of it, she didn't have when she came back out."

Yup, he definitely did more than "glance," Mark thought. "So you saw her leave as well?"

"She wasn't in the apartment long. Just enough time to grab a different coat than the one she was carrying on her arm when she went in. And her purse, I guess." Todd tilted his head. "And I think she brushed her hair out. It was up in a ponytail when she went in."

Awfully observant for someone glancing out a peephole, Mark thought.

Back at the squad room, Mark turned the bagged note into the fingerprinting specialist, the computer into the tech people, then picked up the phone to call Carla's mother. She lived in Lancaster,

Pennsylvania, where Carla had grown up, and he thought a trip there was probably worth getting background information first-hand on Melissa and tracking down the dad angle.

As he was hanging up, his boss entered the office.

"How are you coming on the missing girl case?" Captain McCoy asked.

"I found a note in her room that led to something I need to check out in Lancaster—sent you an email explaining a few minutes ago and a request to fly up there tomorrow. I also want to do some follow up on the guy across the hall, who saw her on the day she disappeared leaving her apartment mid-day."

"Okay, good. Let me know what you find out."

He turned to leave, then turned back around.

"Lancaster, huh? Hey, I have a friend there who can back you up, maybe even help with the investigation."

Both Mark's eyebrows went up.

"I think I can handle this on my own, boss."

Bob laughed.

"I know, Mark. I know. But two heads are always better than one, and I want you to meet this guy. He's a personal friend and a good investigator."

"You've worked with him before?" Mark asked.

"Many times. We were together on the police force in Philly in our early years. But I also worked a couple of cases with him in Lancaster when I was chief there, and he'd started his private eye business."

The captain put both hands behind his head and stretched out the back he was always complaining hurt him.

"Look, I'm not just asking you to visit with this guy because he's a friend. He's been around the block a few times. I think you can learn something by letting him tag along, and he knows that area."

His hands came down and he tapped the front of the desk with one finger, a gesture Mark had learned meant the conversation was over.

"His name is Sam Osborne, and I'll go call him and tell him you're coming."

CHAPTER SIX

Friday, November 11

SAM SMILED at the detective sitting down in the chair on the other side of his desk, trying to get the young man to relax. Mark Brady wasn't nervous, but he acted like he didn't really want to be there. *Maybe he's just all business*, Sam thought.

Bob warned Sam on the phone not to underestimate the abilities or intelligence of the young detective. His friend explained that he sent Mark to Sam not as much to help with the case as to get him around Lancaster and give advice on how to work with the local police department if it came to that. Sam knew the force and its management. He also knew its current leader Delbert Green kept his officers and department resources close to his belt, but that there were ways to get around that reality. One of those ways was Sam's close friend on the force—Danny Jones. Sam had mentored Danny, who was working his way quickly up the ranks of Lancaster's force.

As Sam listened to Mark detail what he knew about the Carla Dunlap case, he took a few moments to study the younger detective. He was about the same height as Sam with dark, curly hair cut short. His boyish, but handsome features included earnest green eyes. His handshake had been firm, which Sam always considered a sign of confidence.

"Welcome to Lancaster," Sam said when Mark paused in his explanation of why he was there. "I hope I can help. Captain McCoy seems to think highly of you."

"Thanks," Mark Brady replied without looking up from the file he was studying. He turned the file around and shoved it across the desk towards Sam as he returned to the case.

"As I was saying, Carla Dunlap's missing persons' report was filed by her roommate Melissa Burns. When I went to the apartment complex where they lived, I interviewed the neighbors, but Carla wasn't well known and only one neighbor reported seeing her the day she disappeared. His comments and what others had to say are right here, and we're working on eliminating the neighbor as a suspect." He leaned across the desk to point out several things, then took out the piece of paper he'd found on the floor.

"This is a copy of the note I found under Carla's desk crumpled in a little ball. Its contents clearly startled Melissa, but led her to admit that Carla recently shared some disturbing news…"

"Dad, eleven-thirty, McDonalds," Sam read after digging out his reading glasses. He said nothing for a moment, then realization hit.

"Wait. I know these Dunlaps. Carla's dad was Charles Dunlap who died a year ago. Is the note that old?"

"No," Mark said. He sat back in his seat and Sam saw him relax for the first time. He was in his element now—sharing the details that made this a mystery.

Mark knitted his fingers together as he explained.

"Carla told Melissa just a day before that there was some question as to whether the man she knew as her father was her natural father—Carla overheard a conversation between her mom and her aunt that lead her to question the situation."

"Ah," Sam said, taking off his glasses and laying them on the papers from the file. "I don't know the Dunlaps well, but enough to attend Charles' funeral. If Carla is adopted or has a different birth father, I don't believe it's general knowledge."

"According to Melissa, it was a shocking revelation to Carla. I need to talk to Mrs. Dunlap and maybe the aunt. It's too much a coincidence that she disappeared right after finding this out and I don't …"

"Believe in coincidence," Sam finished for him.

The two men's eyes met and this time, Mark grinned.

"Exactly," he said.

Sam got up and headed for the coat rack.

"No time like the present," he said. "I believe Mrs. Dunlap will be more comfortable if someone she knows tags along." He put his warmer coat on and added a knitted scarf.

"They're saying it could get nasty out there – a couple of inches of snow." He turned around and offered another scarf from the rack to Mark, who was buttoning up his overcoat.

"Need this?"

"Uh, that's okay. This is a waterproof jacket," the younger man said.

Sam put the scarf back on the rack, and the two men left.

Mark drove his rental, and Sam was impressed at how the other man handled the weather. The snow was coming down heavily, though the roads had only begun to freeze enough to allow accumulation. Mark didn't seem nervous and knew to keep a safe distance from the other cars on the highway. *He must have lived somewhere more north than Richmond to be as relaxed as this in a snowstorm*, Sam thought.

After a twenty-minute drive, Mark parked in the driveway of the Dunlap home. The two men walked up to the door side by side. Sam's secretary Casey Jones had called ahead to make sure Katherine Dunlap knew they were coming.

Carla's mother appeared after only a few raps on the door, her eyes anxious and frightened. "Have you heard anything? Is there news about Carla?" she asked, directing the question towards Sam.

"I'm afraid not," Mark interjected. "I'm Detective Brady from Richmond. I'm looking into her disappearance with Sam's help. We have a few questions."

She didn't reply, but ushered them in with a wave of her hand.

"Haven't seen you since the funeral, Sam," she said, her tone flat. The detectives followed the gray-haired, stocky, and short women into the living room where she invited them to sit. Straightening her shoulders, she took the armchair across from them.

Sam could see the devastation on her face—weary, shaded eyes and wrinkles around the mouth that probably weren't there a few days ago. Although Sam didn't know Katherine well, the woman had been a friend of his ex-wife Barbara. Sam's memory flashed backwards, and he remembered that she'd been supportive of Barbara during the horrible time in Barbara's and Sam's lives right after their son Davie disappeared.

How ironic to be sitting here questioning her about the very same thing—the disappearance of her child, he thought.

"Katherine. We'll do everything we can to find Carla. I promise," he said.

His words only made her eyes fill, but she brushed away her tears before they fell.

"What do you need to know?" she asked, her voice trembling.

"We found a confusing note on her desk," Mark said. He withdrew the duplicate he'd made and handed it over.

She studied the tiny writing, leaned over to the coffee table and picked up her glasses, then studied it again.

Her face turned a sickly white.

"Is this some kind of joke? Charles is dead. He's been gone a year. What does this mean?" She looked up at Sam as if he held the answer.

"I'm sorry," Sam told her. "We don't mean to upset you, but we're trying to understand what's happening here."

Katherine said nothing, but she covered one hand with the other and squeezed, a gesture Sam recognized as nervousness.

"Is there a chance Carla is adopted?" he asked.

"No. No, she's not adopted," she said.

"You're her mother and Charles is her father, then," Mark prodded.

Katherine was studying the knuckles of the top hand, weighing what to say.

"Is there something you need to tell us, Katherine?" Sam said gently.

She didn't acknowledge his comment, but suddenly her shoulders slumped and the tears spilled over.

Sam got up and went to Katherine, laying a calming hand on her shoulder.

"What is it, Katherine?" he said. "Is it something that could help us in this investigation?"

After a few minutes, she calmed, taking in a few breaths to steady herself. Sam took a handkerchief out of his pocket and handed it to Katherine, who grabbed it like it was a life preserver.

Dabbing at her eyes, she said, "I was always sure she was Charles's. She looked and acted so much like him."

The two detectives waited it out, the silence in the room hanging heavily for a few moments. Sam returned to his seat and glanced over at Mark. The other detective seemed to take the same approach he did, which was to wait for a witness to tell his or her story on their own terms and time. *Not many police officers have the patience for that trick*, he thought.

Finally, Katherine sighed and sat back in her chair, clutching the handkerchief with both hands.

"I was brought up to believe that a girl saved herself for her wedding night. My family was religious and so was I—active in the youth group; in church every Sunday."

"Charles was not brought up that way and he was pressuring me for sex, but he respected my wishes. Until one night at a party. I drank punch I didn't know was spiked, and I lost my resolve and my virginity. Charles and I made love in a stranger's bedroom."

She sat rigidly twisting the handkerchief.

"When I awoke several hours later, I was appalled. I acted quite crazy—demanding that Charles marry me immediately."

Despite the tears, Katherine tried to laugh. It turned into another gasp for breath.

"We were so young. I believed I was pregnant right there and then because that's what happened to girls who had sex. Charles was furious and mixed up and … well … he didn't exactly act chivalrously. He got up, got dressed and left me there alone to deal with the devastation."

She untwisted the handkerchief then and used the flattened cloth to wipe her face.

"The next few weeks I heard nothing from him, and I went crazy with anger and fear. I'd been a good little girl all my life and now here I was—in disgrace and pregnant. I couldn't tell my parents; we didn't have that kind of family relationship. So I went out and I found a couple guys and I got my revenge. Figured I deserved a little fun before they packed me off to an unwed mothers' home."

"But Charles came back into the picture," Sam said.

Katherine nodded her head and stared at her lap.

"He's Charles. He always needed time to process change or shocking news, but he was a good man. I was, indeed pregnant, but he married me, and I got my little family."

Her eyes rose now to meet Sam's.

"Once I learned you don't get pregnant right away, I wondered about those other two guys."

She got up from the chair and went to a desk in the alcove. Sam could hear her ruffling through drawers.

When she returned she handed Mark a piece of paper.

"Their names and the last addresses I had for them—both were local bad boys at the time this all happened. Neither ended up that way. Peter Grindage still lives in the area and has a successful business. I know what he's been up to because I know his sister, June. She and I were classmates and pretty good friends. She now lives in Richmond, and I gave Carla her contact information. The two of them—June and Carla—kept in touch and had coffee I think.

"Don Thomas moved to Arizona after graduation—that address is probably old. I did befriend him on Facebook a couple of years ago. But I haven't seen any postings for a long time."

Her head snapped up.

"Neither of these men know about that time in my life, or this situation. I don't want you telling them if it can be avoided."

"I don't see why that would be necessary unless we find out they are involved somehow," Mark said softly. "We may want to chat with June, though, since she lives there in Richmond and has been in touch with Carla."

"Thank you for this information," Sam said. "I know it was hard for you to share it. But I have one more important question: did your husband or daughter know about this?"

"Oh, no," she said, shaking her head. "I never told Charles, and I certainly didn't tell Carla. The only person who knew was my sister Bethany. She's always been my confessor."

"Would you mind giving us her name and number? Like I said, we believe Carla heard you two talking. But maybe Bethany also told someone else," Sam said.

"Oh, she'd never do that." She reached for the piece of paper, however, and wrote down the information. "She'll back me up on that."

Mark and Sam rose to leave but Katherine stopped Sam with a hand on his forearm.

"Sam, I know you'll do what you can to help Detective Brady here, but I'd like to assure that you have that ability. I'd like to hire you in an official capacity. I have plenty of money left over from Charles's life insurance, and I can't think of a better use for it than to bring my daughter home."

Sam smiled and nodded his head. He didn't really care about her money, but she needed his help.

"I'll find out where she is," he said.

By the time Sam and Mark were back on the road, the snow had stopped and the sun was shining. The two decided to stop by Pete's Mechanical Magic shop, the repair business started by Peter Grindage. The shop was in a booming industrial park and took up two large, side-by-side spaces.

Although he'd been wild in his youth, Katherine had reported that Pete grew up to take over his dad's auto repair shop and found he had a knack for running a business. A smaller, one-bay shop in a run-down neighborhood had morphed into this successful facility in a newer location.

Carla had been gone only a few days, and the media hadn't gotten wind of the situation. Unless he was involved, it was unlikely Pete had heard what happened. Katherine also reported that while she and Pete's sister, June, remained friends, the two women hadn't seen each other in a while.

After telling the young man working reception they were there, the man talked into his phone, and they heard Pete being called to the office.

When Mark flashed his badge several minutes later, Pete's eyes narrowed. He motioned them into his private office behind the reception area.

"What is it? Is one of my employees in trouble?" the balding sixty-something man plopped his pear-shaped body onto an office chair.

Mark and Sam took seats opposite his desk.

"Not that we know of," Mark replied. "This is about someone you know—a Katherine Dunlap."

Sam watched for a change of expression or demeanor. All he saw was concern.

"My sister's friend?" Pete asked. "Is she all right? Has something happened with Katherine?"

"No. It's her daughter Carla," Mark said. The statement lingered in the air, and Sam realized Mark was using the technique again—waiting to see how Pete would react before explaining further.

Pete's concern morphed into confusion.

"Why are you questioning me about Katherine's daughter?"

Interesting, Sam thought. He hadn't asked what happened, just why *he* was being questioned.

But Sam had promised Katherine not to bring up the father angle unless he had to, so he took charge of the conversation.

"Carla Dunlap is missing. Katherine Dunlap has hired me to look into it," he said. "While Detective Brady is here in Lancaster, we're questioning anyone in town who knows the family. Katherine said she and your sister June were good friends."

All of Pete's attention went from Mark to Sam.

"You're not with the police?" he asked.

"I'm a private investigator working with Katherine and the police. Mark's with the Richmond police so he's here gathering information."

Pete's shoulders relaxed, and he leaned back in his chair.

"Yes, June and Katherine have been friends many years. Ever since we were all in high school together. That's terrible about Katherine's daughter. What can I do to help?"

"When was the last time you saw Carla Dunlap?" he asked.

The confusion returned.

"I think I met her once when Katherine came into her shop with her husband and daughter. But that was many years ago—she was just a girl."

"And you haven't seen her since then?"

Pete ran his thumb and forefinger around his lips and plopped that hand down on his desk.

"Didn't I just say that?"

Mark jumped into the conversation.

"We are just trying to establish if anyone living around here, her hometown, has seen Carla lately. We'll stop by your sister's house when we're back in Richmond and talk to other people Katherine said Carla knows. So you haven't seen Carla for a while. What about Katherine? When's the last time you were in contact with Katherine?"

Pete sat back in his chair and frowned.

"Why is this important?" he asked.

"It's a standard question," Mark said. "While we're here in Lancaster, I'm talking to as many people as I can who know the family."

That seemed to mollify Pete. He didn't need to know that they were only now getting into the investigation. Pete drummed his fingers on the desk, thinking.

"Probably Charles' funeral. I went with June to pay my respects."

A knock on the door interrupted their conversation. The head of the young man from reception popped into the office.

"Mrs. Haster is going ballistic, Boss. You think you could come talk to her?"

Pete sighed as if the pronouncement was a heavy burden he had to bear. He got slowly to his feet and came around the desk.

"I'm afraid I need to go, gentleman. Mrs. Haster won't talk to anyone but me, and I don't have much to help you with anyway. I barely know Mrs. Dunlap. I am assuming you'll get more from my sister."

"Sure," Mark said. "Thanks for your time." The detectives rose and left.

In the car, Mark and Sam turned towards each other and Sam knew they were thinking the same thing.

If he was at the funeral, wouldn't he have seen Carla then? Why wouldn't that have come to mind when they asked about the last time he'd seen her?

Bethany James was tall and slim and looked nothing like her sister. She had an air of crispness that contrasted sharply with the worn feel of Katherine Dunlap. Instead of grey hair and a few extra pounds, she was blonde and almost too thin.

She was more than willing to share what she knew, and Sam was surprised at how readily she chatted about her sister's personal life. Gossip didn't seem to go with the professional image she portrayed—a bank manager living in a large McMansion in one of Lancaster's elite neighborhoods. Maybe she was discreet on the job. But she wasn't afraid to spill the beans on her sister.

"I just couldn't believe that Katherine slept with two men before she married Charles. It was enough of a family disgrace that she *had* to get married," Bethany said. They were all seated in what Sam assumed from its beige sterility was a rarely used formal living room.

Although her chattiness didn't seem to fit the formalness, Sam didn't think from her tone that she was being judgmental. She sounded more fascinated than disgusted, and she wasn't looking at either of her visitors. She was peering at her own coffee table as if it held old family secrets.

Perhaps Katherine had been the tamer of the two when they were teens, Sam thought.

Bethany smiled then and caught Sam's eye.

"Her pregnancy seemed tragic at the time. But these days, that would mean *nothing,*" she said.

"You're probably right," Sam said. "Why did she decide to tell you now, after all these years, about the other guys? What prompted the conversation?"

Bethany blushed slightly.

"Alcohol, I'm afraid. We've recently decided —well since Charles death—that we deserved one night out a month without the pressures of our daily life. I need it because, well, I hate my job. She just needs to let go of the tragedy of the last year and have fun. We went to Benihana and consumed about three sakes each. Enough that we took a cab to her home where we continued to bare our souls, helped along by a few glasses of wine."

The briefly upturned corners of her mouth that accompanied her recollections of the past disappeared and her facial features stiffened.

"I just can't believe Carla heard us talking and found out that way. I swear I would never tell anyone. I just pray to God this didn't contribute to what's happened. That she hasn't run off somewhere."

Bethany swiped her brow.

"God, where is she?"

"What sort of relationship did Carla have with her dad … I mean Charles of course," Sam said.

Bethany straightened in her chair and joined her hands.

"Carla has always been close to both parents."

She placed her joined hands on one knee and took in a breath, letting it out slowly.

"That's why this had to have been a shock to her; the man she thought was her father might not even be her father!"

"So, do you think she may have pursued finding out who *was* her biological father?" Mark asked.

Bethany turned his way.

"Absolutely. I mean, I didn't even know she'd found out so I can't really say how she'd react to this particular thing. But I know how much this must have upset her … thrown her off course. She's a stubborn gal when it comes to a lot of things. If she had a lead on who he might be, I can see her pursuing it."

CHAPTER SEVEN

WHEN SAM AND HIS WIFE Maggie invited Mark to have dinner in their home that night, he gladly accepted, not anxious to spend a lonely evening at his hotel with a take-out pizza. He wasn't flying home until the next day.

When Maggie opened the front door to the two detectives, Mark was struck first by the unusual deep violet of her eyes and second by the twinkle they contained. She drew Sam into a hug then motioned the two into the Osborne home with a warmth that matched Sam's friendly nature and reminded Mark of his own sister.

Mark felt instantly comfortable in the cottage-style house. It wasn't large, but the rooms had a feeling of spaciousness helped along by high ceilings.

A quick tour of the home showed Mark that the Osbornes had an eclectic taste for both comfort and quality with a blend of antiques and soft furnishings such as colorful rugs on hardwood floors and bright draperies in the room where they ended the tour. He relaxed easily into one of the velvety easy chairs and was offered a beer or a glass of wine. He chose the beer, as did both Sam and his wife.

As the three of them chatted, Mark studied the couple. Maggie and Sam were both trim and looked like they kept in shape, but Maggie was tall for a woman while Sam might have been considered short. The result was that they stood almost exactly eye to eye.

They seemed totally relaxed hosting a stranger; they knew how to draw Mark into their world through entertaining tales while drawing him out of his own shell with questions about his background.

What struck him most, however, was the way they interacted with each other.

While Maggie went back and forth from living room to kitchen to fetch the beers and then crackers and cheese, she was never far from Sam's side when she was in the room and seemed to need to touch him periodically. She perched on the arm of his chair or sat across from him, leaning forward to pat his knee when he made a point. Once they were seated at the dining room table, Sam took her hand and pulled her over for a kiss on the cheek and a "thank you" for the dinner. It was a simple, but delicious meal of roast beef, succulent rosemary-scented potatoes, and glazed carrots.

What struck Mark most as he savored his food and continued studying them was the deep connection he felt between the two—they were like two sides to the same coin. They were very different faces of the coin, but they seemed to work together to create value. Would he ever find that kind of connection with a woman?

"I'm sorry you didn't get to meet Jenna," Maggie said, interrupting his thoughts. "She loves visitors and probably would have shown you all her American Girl dolls and talked your ear off."

Jenna was the couple's only child—Maggie's by blood, Sam's by adoption.

Mark listened as the couple talked about the amazing story of their unusual daughter. The girl had been kidnapped at an early age, and Jenna's case was how Sam and Maggie had met. Maggie hired Sam, who tracked the little girl down to an Amish area in Ohio where she lived for several years.

"My Jenna came to believe that she was there with the couple because I was in mortal danger," Maggie said as she sipped a final cup of coffee.

"When we found her, she kept saying she always knew I'd come for her. It's really quite amazing she came out of all that with very few emotional scars."

Sam swallowed his bite of chocolate mousse and added: "We've even allowed her to keep in touch with and visit the Amish couple where the kidnapper hid her away."

"You're kidding," Mark couldn't help saying. He'd forgone both the coffee and the mousse, stuffed to the gills.

Sam laughed and set his fork down.

"I know that sounds crazy. But the couple weren't really the kidnappers. They'd been told she was a child in need of a home, and they tried to give her that home."

Maggie gave her mouth a tap with her napkin.

"Jenna is talented at recognizing people with good hearts," she said. "She's even brought out the best in my ex." She grinned and rose to begin clearing the table. Mark stood up as well, insisting on helping her clean up.

After the dishes were tucked into the dishwasher, Mark yawned and told them it was time for him to get to his hotel.

As Mark was putting on his coat to leave, Maggie brought Jenna's name up again.

"Hopefully next time you visit, we'll have our Jenna here to entertain you. This is one of her dad's weeks. Say, are you *sure* you wouldn't be more comfortable staying with us?"

"The dinner was wonderful. The conversation entertaining. And thank you for that offer. Like you said earlier; maybe next visit, Maggie. Thanks for a relaxing evening," Mark said.

Sam walked Mark to his car and stood for moment, sharing a few last thoughts about their case.

"Before we delve deeper tomorrow into the facts and the players, what are your initial thoughts about Carla?" Sam asked his new friend.

Mark let his thoughts ferment for just a moment. He turned toward Sam when he was ready with an answer.

"I think a planner is behind this and that she was taken. I don't think this is random. She goes to meet with a man she thinks is her father. Heck, maybe it *is* one of the men who could be her father. And she doesn't return to meet up with her roommate even though she's already indicated she needs to talk."

"This whole thing has something to do with that note," Mark concluded.

Sam was nodding his head.

"I agree, and if I'm going to be working for Katherine, I need to start there. I'll follow up with her roommate Melissa, then maybe talk to some of her professors. Since Pete's sister June lives outside of Richmond and is Katherine's friend, why don't I make my way to your neck of the woods and talk to her. I'll probably drive it maybe tomorrow after we finish here. That okay with you?"

Mark's put his key in his rental car door then turned back and smiled.

"Of course, Sam. It's my turn to play host and introduce you to the guys on the force. And I'll want be part of your conversation with June Grindage. Thanks for dinner. I'll see you at your office at eight."

Saturday, November 12

The next morning at Sam's office, he introduced Mark to Danny Jones, his friend on the Lancaster force and also his secretary's husband. Danny, a tall, imposing man with startling blue eyes and coal black hair, contrasted sharply with his petite blonde, wheelchair-bound wife, Casey. Mark felt another stab of envy as he watched the camaraderie that flowed between Sam, Danny, and Casey. Coffee in the morning was obviously a frequent occurrence and the three chatted amiably like long-time friends do. Danny was dressed in his uniform, ready to leave for his shift.

They sat for a while in Sam's office, and the conversation turned towards the case. Danny had come to the office armed with information on the Grindage family as well as the Dunlaps and Carla's neighbor Todd. He must have done some research the night before as a favor for Sam, Mark thought. He wondered if Sam knew how fortunate he was as a private investigator to have such a good tie-in to the police department.

"The local man Pete may have an alibi for where he was when Carla disappeared—in that shop of his. He apparently works long hours, and we talked to several employees who said he was in the shop all day this week. We haven't located the guy who moved out West—Don Thomas. Still tracking him down. I did a preliminary search on Todd Walker,

Carla's neighbor and found no record of criminal activity and no flags so far."

Danny left around eight for his shift and Mark spent the next few hours trying to track down any Don Thomases in Arizona.

"There are forty-eight Don Thomases listed in the white pages in Arizona," Mark said, staring at his computer screen. "Thirty-nine of them have drivers' licenses and four of them have criminal records."

He ran his hand over his mouth and leaned in a little closer to peer at his screen.

"Of those that have driver's license, fifteen would be about the right age. That should help us out."

Sam put a mug of steaming coffee in front of Mark, who looked up briefly and muttered a "thanks."

"Any of those that have records look like they might have a tie-in?" he asked.

Mark's focus was back on the screen, his hand clutching the mouse.

"Not really. Minor theft. Sexual misconduct—but that guy is too old. Here's one for insider trading. I don't see how any of those connect." He sat back and took a sip of his coffee.

"And what about Peter Grindage?" Mark asked Sam.

"Mike's Mechanical Magic Shop is a booming business," Sam said, flipping through the paperwork

Danny had left. He sat down across from Mark, his hands encircling his own mug.

"The business currently employs a dozen mechanics and gets great reviews. Danny managed to talk to a few local businesses and a couple of his customers to see what kind of reputation the place has. Pete is known for being fair to customers and unwilling to sacrifice safety for customers' pocketbooks."

Sam laughed as he added, "Course none of that has anything to do with a missing girl, but it does tell us he's *not* known for his shiftiness."

"Why don't you run off that white pages listing and whatever else you find about the Don Thomases in Arizona," he continued. "I'll have Casey check against social media and see if she comes up with anything."

Mark picked up his cell phone to check the time.

"I'll leave it here on the screen for her, but I've also sent the info to my Richmond office for follow up. Speaking of which, I should head back home. My plane leaves in an hour."

It was about ten-thirty in the morning and Sam had already indicated he'd be driving to Richmond a few hours after Mark left.

Mark rose, gathered his files and packed it all in his briefcase. He was saying his goodbyes to Casey when his cell phone rang.

Mark saw that it was the Richmond police office and held up a finger towards Casey to indicate he had to take the call.

"Yes, sir. I was just about ready to go to the airport. There's a flight in an hour."

"Glad I caught you," Bob McCoy said. "I have another situation you need to check out—and maybe Sam can get you there."

Mark grabbed a notebook laying on Casey's desk and took a pen out of his pocket.

"There's been a disappearance reported in Winchester, Virginia—a woman, around forty-five years old. Husband said she went to the store for an errand and never returned. Name's Alice Springer."

Mark glanced at Sam, who was standing in his office door threshold. Sam had his hand on the doorknob as though he was about to close the office door. Mark's sudden animation stopped him.

"It probably has nothing to do with the University of Richmond situation, and it's not in our jurisdiction, but I've already talked to police there," Bob continued "I think you should see if there are any similarities."

Mark turned the notebook around towards Sam. It read: *Missing woman, Alice Springer. Disappeared from store Thursday. Winchester.* Can you take me? he mouthed. Sam nodded.

"Yes, sir. Sam was driving back to Richmond with me to interview Katherine Dunlap's sister—we can go via Winchester. Mrs. Dunlap has retained Sam to look into the Carla Dunlap thing, but I'm sure he wouldn't mind helping with Winchester."

Mark heard his captain chuckle.

"Of course. And it will be good to see my old friend. I'll send the details to your email address."

Mark ended the call and walked back with Sam into his office to check his email and run off what his boss had sent. The two men sat flipping through the few sheets of paper.

"Hmmm. Went to the store last minute to pick up supplies for a baby shower she was hosting," Mark said.

"Yeah, doesn't sound like your typical wife skipping out on the family," Sam added.

Their eyes met.

"So how do we connect a college student in Richmond with a woman on a fast trip to the local neighborhood mart?" Sam said.

"We probably don't. But two women that close together in when they disappeared is something worth looking into. I'm glad Winchester police are willing to work with us," Mark said. He picked up one of the pieces of paper.

"I guess we start where police probably started and talk to the family."

"I need to make a quick call to Maggie," Sam said. "Then if you don't mind, after we leave Winchester, I'll drop you off at Dulles Airport in D.C. and head back here. Tomorrow is Sunday and I don't miss that day with the family unless I absolutely have to. I'll head to Richmond Monday."

Mark gave Sam the address of the Springer family and the detectives entered it into Sam's GPS system.

CHAPTER EIGHT

WINCHESTER IS A QUIET TOWN with that solid, established feel that comes from tree-lined streets filled with well-kept newer homes sprinkled among grand old homes.

George and Alice Springer owned one of the newer houses, a three-level split built in the 1980s or 1990s that was neither the most elegant nor the smallest on the street. The lawn was immaculately manicured; the pale yellow house well maintained with freshly painted shutters and bushes resting up against the base level.

The two detectives strolled side by side up the flower-lined sidewalk.

The woman who opened the door was tall and buxom with brown eyes and hair, and for a split second, Mark thought Alice had returned home. Then he realized he was looking at a younger version with a little less weight and no wrinkles. She had to be Alice's daughter, Mary.

The anxious face of an older man appeared over her shoulder and his red rimmed eyes and expectant look convinced Mark this was probably George, Alice's husband. The man saw Mark flash his badge, then turned and stormed away.

Mary ushered them into the living room, then joined her father on the couch, patting his knee.

When Sam and Mark were seated across from them in matching armchairs, Mark began.

"Your mother has disappeared," he said. Mary nodded her head.

"Isn't that why you're here?" George interjected. "Another couple of cops asking questions. She's been gone for two days and we've heard *nothing.*"

Mark cleared his throat, then kept his tone even, but firm.

"I know how frustrating this is, Mr. Springer. I'm sorry to be adding to your burden, but Sam and I are from different jurisdictions than the local police. We are coming at this from another angle altogether and anything you can tell us might help. We'll work with local police in the effort to find your wife."

"Another angle?" George asked. Mark ignored the question. It wasn't time for them to share why they'd traveled from Richmond to Winchester.

"Can you please go over some of the details again? You may think of something new as we talk. Let's start with: when did you last see her and what was her state of mind?"

"My wife was in a perfectly good *state of mind*," George said. He was holding his middle and rocking slightly forward and backward.

"I know how you cops think, and I know the husband is the first one everyone suspects, but my wife was *taken*. Some goddamn pervert has kidnapped her and here we all are, sitting around waiting for something to happen while we answer the same questions over and over."

Awful lot of anger and defensiveness in the man, Mark thought. *Was Alice trying to escape something?*

Mary was more composed, sitting straight-backed on the couch, her fingers knitted together and resting in her lap.

"Mother was dressed and ready for the baby shower she was hosting for a friend of mine," she interjected.

Mark began taking notes.

"She suddenly remembered she'd forgotten to get extra ice. I wasn't dressed yet so Mom said she would run to Weiss' Market and get it. That was about four. The party was to start at six," she said.

The calm demeanor crumbled a little, and she began to rub her cheeks as if trying to keep the tears at bay.

"If I'd been dressed … If I'd gone for the ice myself, maybe she'd still be here!"

"You can't know that, Mary. It does no good to think like that," Mark said softly.

Mary sniffled, and her calm was restored.

"When she didn't come back by five, we started calling her cell phone. When the time for the party came, and went, Dad called the police. We turned our guests away at the door, though a few insisted on staying for support."

One shaky hand came up to comb through her hair.

"Thirty minutes later, the police were at our door, reporting that the car was still in the parking lot—empty," she said.

"There was a plastic sack of melting ice in the back seat," George added. His voice caught at the end, and he clenched his fists until he was white-knuckled. His chest rose and fell in quick, jerky motions, and Mary reached out to touch her father's arm.

"No," he barked at her, then seeing her wince, whispered, "It just isn't right." He shut his eyes and breathed deeply, forcing his shoulders to relax.

"She went into the store and bought the ice," George said. His eyes snapped open. "She just didn't make it back here. They checked under the hood. The guy had disabled her car battery—loosened one of the cables. She wouldn't have even known what to look for. Why didn't she call me if the car wouldn't start?" He was clenching his fists again.

"I'm sorry to ask this, but has your wife ever disappeared like this before?" Mark asked.

"Like I told the other policeman, *of course* not!" George's words were clipped.

"No, never," Mary added.

"And it's not possible she'd be involved with another man or taken off somewhere with a friend?" Mark continued.

"That's absolutely ridiculous!" George barked. "My wife was not some bored housewife, running around on her husband. She didn't even like sex!"

Mary threw her father a disgusted glare, and George seemed to realize what he'd said. His mouth shut into a tight line, and he clasped his hands together to steady them.

Sam turned to Mary.

"Tell me about your mom," Sam said. Mark recognized what Sam was doing: throwing out an open-ended question often yielded more information than the standard queries.

Mary rubbed at her brow while her eyes drifted around the room as if searching for the answer. Her gaze lingered on the family portrait hanging above the mantle. In the picture George sat stiff and unsmiling. A much younger Mary stood at his side, wearing layers of pink ruffles and a puckish grin. His wife stood just behind him, her hand resting on his shoulder, her crisp formal blouse a contrast to her relaxed expression.

The picture seemed to deepen Mary's frown.

"I used to tease Mom that she was Donna Reed from that old TV show, right down to the house dress. She really didn't much care for the jeans or khakis most mothers wore—she tended to skirts and blouses even around the house. My friends used to tease me, but I didn't care."

She breathed in slowly, held her breath, then released it in a whoosh, dropping her shoulders.

"She was a great mother and a really good housewife. She always said it was her profession—taking care of Dad and me."

Mark referred to the notes he'd brought along.

"It says here she was wearing an apron when she went to the store. She was really that old fashioned?"

Mary smiled weakly.

"That was actually her pride and joy. I bought it as a joke—the frilly apron of Donna Reed. But she wore it anyway—especially to any parties she threw."

Suddenly, George's fist crashed on the coffee table, drawing all eyes his way.

"Why—why would anyone take my Alice? She's just a middle-aged housewife for God's sake!"

Mary reached over and laid her palm on his fist.

"They'll find her, Dad," she said. "She'll be okay."

The neighbors that lived in the Springer neighborhood had mostly positive things to say about George and Alice Springer. One young couple laughingly called them the Cleavers after the old television show Leave it to Beaver—the apron probably contributed to the image. Mark could tell, however, that the reference was not used with scorn—the men in the neighborhood praised George for how well he kept up with his lawn and several mentioned getting house maintenance tips from him, and in one case, help in making a repair. Both men and women talked about Alice's penchant for stopping by with a casserole when someone was ill or grieving. It was clear that the neighbors considered the Springers old-fashioned, but good people with a streak of kindness.

That is, until the detectives talked to the couple across the street—Hester and Homer Brown.

Without much prompting, Hester Brown launched into a negative assessment of her neighbors.

"I've long suspected that couple is not what they seem. I've seen bruises on Alice's wrists. She probably ran away."

The tall, thin woman looked down on Mark and Sam from a height at least three inches over either of them. She was like a tall tree, straight up and down with a full head of gray foliage topping the image.

Unlike some of the other neighbors, she didn't invite the detectives inside, but stood at the door spouting information without much prompting. So far, Mark had only showed his badge and asked if they knew the Springers.

"I've also seen George Springer sneak out at night," Hester continued. "I'm sure he's cheating on her, and he even brought the floozy home when Alice was off shopping."

Homer Brown appeared at her side. Homer was as wide as Hester was tall with no hair on his head, but a thick grey beard. He looked like he'd just woken from a nap.

"Let the gentlemen in for a moment, Hester," he said.

When the four were settled in the living room, Mark turned to Homer.

"Do you agree with your wife's assessment of the couple?" he asked.

Homer seemed confused for a second, as if he wasn't used to being the one in this couple to answer questions.

"Well, I can't say that I've noticed much about them. I leave that to my wife. If she says it's true about George and Alice, it's true."

"That's not all," Hester interrupted. "That daughter is just as bad. She treats Alice horribly—lives with them still at twenty-four and lets her mom clean up after her and cook for her. I've seen Mary Springer let her mother carry all the groceries in without lending a hand. Poor woman, to be treated so badly by her family. Someone ought to have done something about it is what I say."

Mark took out a notebook as much to draw the rampaging Hester's attention away from her tirade of venom as to take notes. It worked. The woman's eyes flew to the paper, and she stopped talking.

"So, you've seen Mr. Springer and this woman he's cheating with together at the house?" Mark prompted.

"Of course," she answered, drawing herself up, her eyes still glued to the notebook.

"On multiple occasions?" he asked.

Hester glared at Mark as if the question was completely irrelevant and an insult to her intelligence. She sniffed and continued.

"As I said, he brought his woman to the house when Alice was off shopping or at the doctors or something," she said.

"I don't know her name, but I know she works at Prudential Real Estate. She has one of those magnetic signs on her car, which I've seen several times parked at the curb."

She crossed her legs at the ankle and rested back against her chair like she'd just settled the matter.

"I've also seen her going into the Prudential office, which is right next door to my dentist on Maple," she said.

"Can you describe this women's physical appearance?" Sam said. Hester glanced his way as though seeing him for the first time.

"She looks like you'd expect such a woman to look," she said.

"And that would be …?" Sam prompted.

"Strawberry blonde hair. Lots of make-up. Short skirt. Tight sweater. Red shoes."

Sam seemed to be suppressing a smile and Mark understood his amusement. She remembered the woman's shoe color? Hester obviously had something against George or men in general or maybe women who dressed too sexy.

Before she could go into another tirade, Mark thanked her and closed the notebook. They weren't getting much else out of this woman, and her assessment was so different than everyone else's that he tended to disregard her scorn. He and Sam could check out the real estate office to see if they could find the blonde woman with the red shoes.

Ten minutes later, after hearing similar warnings from Hester against several other neighbors, the detectives were at the curb. Sam snickered and turned to Mark.

"Wow. She's something else, huh?"

"I do believe that she is the most extremely unpleasant 'witness' I've ever interviewed," Mark replied. "I wonder if Homer ever gets a word in?"

They laughed together.

"Think there's any truth to her claims?" Mark said.

"No. Not really. But while we're here, let's stop by Prudential in the business center Hester named and see if we can track down this woman," Sam said.

"It's not likely the Winchester police had time or the patience to track down the 'floozy' Hester is so obsessed with, so maybe we'll find out something," Sam added. "If it's true she's been there multiple times, she obviously knows the family."

The woman in question was easy to locate since the small office had only a handful of employees, and only one was blonde and female. The detectives were lucky she wasn't in the field because Ingrid Johannsen was a real estate agent.

She was, indeed, a striking woman whose fitted suit showed off a shapely figure. However, Mark noted that while her clothes fit snugly, she didn't come across as unprofessional or trashy.

"Yes, I know George Springer," she said. Mark detected a slight accent. "He's a distant cousin. I was born in Sweden and came here when I was about ten. Our grandmothers reconnected in this country. They're sisters, which I guess makes George a second cousin."

The three were sitting in a small, but neatly organized office—no stray piles of paper on the desk, only a few mementoes on the book shelves. On the walls were several certificates that indicated Ingrid was a top seller for her firm.

"Actually, we've had this argument several times. George says first cousin once removed." She smiled to herself. "I looked it up a while ago, but haven't bothered to let him know."

"Are you involved romantically with George?" Mark asked. He knew the question was blunt, but his instinct told him not to waste anyone's time trying to be discreet.

After the question had a minute to settle, Ingrid burst into laughter.

"Mrs. Brown, right?"

The detectives didn't reply.

"It has to be Mrs. Brown. That woman practically glares at me every time I go over there.

"George and I really don't spend a lot of time together," she explained. "But a couple of months ago, I was sneaking over during the day to help George plan a surprise birthday party for Alice. I'm afraid I got a little tired of seeing Hester's disapproving frown peeking out from behind the curtain."

The gleam in her eye was what Mark would have called "deliciously devilish," especially given the circumstances.

"I'm afraid I may have played it up a bit. I gave it my best saunter up the sidewalk and managed to plant a kiss on his cheek when I left. I don't think George even knew what I was doing, but I frankly didn't care. The woman is not a neighborhood favorite, and I'm sure I'm not the only one who gets the creeps at her peering out at them."

After a few more minutes, Mark and Sam thanked her for her time. At the front door she turned to face both men directly. Her expression had settled into complete seriousness.

"Look. It's terrible what you've told me about Alice going missing. I can't imagine what George and Mary are going through. I don't spend much time with the family, but they're relatives, and I'll be sure to call and lend my support.

"But one thing I'm very sure about. Alice may be a bit old fashioned, but George seems to care about her deeply. He had nothing to do with this."

"Thank you, Ms. Johannsen. We appreciate your time and insight," Mark said.

The two men walked out to the car. Before he got into the passenger side, Mark turned to Sam.

"One thing Hester Brown said rang true at least …"

Sam's eyebrows rose.

"She does like red shoes."

The two men laughed together again.

The store where Alice Springer was last seen was a small grocer—the kind where people went for certain items because the owner would keep them in stock for neighbors or where you ran out in bedroom slippers for a loaf of bread. It was known for its butcher shop and a fresh bakery, but people didn't buy toilet paper in quantity there.

"I can't believe Mrs. Springer has gone missing," Harvey Metzger was smoothing out imaginary wrinkles in his butcher's apron. The short, balding man explained that he'd not been in the night Alice went missing, but was on the premises most days.

"Did she come here often then?" Mark asked.

Harvey's hands stopped stroking, and he picked up the rag hanging over his shoulder to wipe his sweaty forehead.

"Oh, yeah. A couple times a week maybe. She had me double cut her stew meat into smaller pieces. She treated herself to a donut on Saturday mornings. Wasn't here this morning of course." Harvey shook his head, his eyes heavy with sadness.

"Taken right from our parking lot. Right here in our neighborhood. This can't be happening," he muttered.

The detectives were a little luckier with the clerk—Marta Evan. She'd been working the day Alice disappeared and had waited on her.

"She only got that one bag of ice and she seemed to be in a hurry," Marta said. She reached up to run one hand through the black, wispy hair that barely covered her bright red scalp. The woman seemed pleased to be questioned about what happened.

"Was she with someone or did she seem nervous or anxious?" he asked. Mark saw her glance at Harvey, who was watching them all. She began stocking the candy rack by the cash register like she needed to look busy.

"Oh not at all. In a hurry, yeah, but she seemed happy and relaxed. Was chatting it up with the guy behind her; it kind of felt like they were old friends or something."

Sam and Mark exchanged a glance.

"Do you know the gentleman that was behind her?" Mark asked. Marta's hand hovered over a rack, a few bars of candy clutched in her fist. She pursed her lips to think.

"Nope. I mean, I recognized him. I think he'd been in a couple times, but just recently, like in the last couple of weeks. He wasn't one of my regulars though."

She cracked her gum as she continued putting candy down.

"When he checked out, I noticed he went out to a car I assumed was his since he stuck his key in the lock. It was parked right next to Mrs. Springer's. They were continuing their conversation out there. I swear they seemed like old friends." Finished with the candy, Marta straightened up her counter, glanced at her boss again and turned to face Mark and Sam, her attention now fully on them.

"Have you seen the man since that day?" Mark asked

"No," Marta said. She pursed her lips again. "Hey, that's kind of suspicious, isn't it? Do you think he was the kidnapper?"

"We don't even know that she was kidnapped, but we're covering all angles," Mark said. "Can you describe the guy?"

"There isn't much to describe. He kind of seemed like somebody's daddy, khakis, and a button-down collar shirt. Brown hair, I think. Ordinary features. Not short, not tall. Pretty well built though."

Her eyes suddenly lit up.

"Say, do you need me to come down to the station and describe him to an artist. I think I can do that you know."

"Since your store cameras are not working, the Winchester police may ask you to do that. We're only here for information. Did he pay with a credit card or check?" Mark asked.

"Nah. He paid in cash. I think he paid in cash the other times he came in, too. Any more, that's unusual," she said.

"And what did he buy?" Sam asked.

Marta had to think about that one. It didn't do much good.

"I don't really remember. A loaf of bread? Some milk? Food mostly, I think."

Mark handed her a card.

"If you think of anything else …"

"Yeah, sure," she said.

After dropping Mark at Dulles airport, Sam headed back to Lancaster, thinking about what he and Maggie would do tomorrow. Sunday was their date day and no matter how busy either of them got, they spent as many Sundays as they could by doing things they called "celebrations of life"—watching a play they'd been wanting to see, horseback riding in the country, visiting old friends they'd been missing.

He needed this Sunday in particular. The cases already had him wound too tightly after only two days. There was little else Sam hated more in his line of work than working on missing persons. It hit too close to the greatest tragedy of his life: the disappearance of his son.

Sam recognized the hollowness in the unfocused eyes of George Springer, the tightly drawn together lips, the nervous play of his hands. Sam saw the devastation on Katherine Dunlap's face—felt her helplessness and the battle against despair that she was slowly losing.

The two were terrified of what could be happening to their loved ones.

Mark was also thinking about Sunday. He would spend it like he spent many others: Sunday dinner with his sister Janet. A ballgame on the television. An afternoon nap to make up for the sleep he'd missed during the week.

Somehow this week, it didn't feel like enough. He pictured the easy comradery Sam had with his secretary Casey and her husband Danny. He saw again Maggie sitting on the chair arm, bending over to give Sam a quick smooch before getting up to return to the kitchen.

He was too raw from having lost his mother; too alone from having just started to know his fellow detectives and police officers. He knew the friendships would come eventually, and as far as romance, it wasn't like he'd dated much in the hectic years of school. So what was he missing?

The red curls of Melissa Burns appeared in his head. What would she do on a Saturday night or a Sunday? Study? Did she have a boyfriend?

Why the hell are you even thinking about this?

Fraternizing with a possible witness outside the office was *not* a good idea.

Maybe we could go for coffee, though.

"You're such an idiot," Mark said to the darkness outside his plane window.

CHAPTER NINE

Sunday, November 13

EVERY SUNDAY since he'd been on his own, Mark's sister Janet had come to visit or invited him to her house to catch up on the happenings of the week. He knew she counted on this and so did he. A weekly assessment of where they were in their lives.

Janet's car was in his driveway at eleven-thirty sharp, which meant she'd come straight from church. She was without her husband Ben and their children so she must have needed an afternoon off.

By twelve-thirty, delicious smells were wafting from his kitchen, causing Mark's mouth to water. He ate too many frozen dinners or hurriedly picked up food that he ate straight from cardboard containers.

It was one of the things he appreciated the most about Sundays: a home-cooked meal. He also appreciated the fact Janet made a big deal of setting the table properly, getting out the napkins (even if they were only paper), real dishes and glassware. It reminded him of Sundays when they were little, and the family gathered for ham or roast chicken. He pictured his dad carving and his mom serving.

Guess I could use a few more friends who can cook or I need to learn to cook myself, Mark admitted to himself. But he also knew how lucky he was to have Janet as a sister since she fit both the friend and cook category.

"Dinner is ready," Janet called from the kitchen. "Wash up and meet me at the table in five minutes."

Mark grinned and turned off the football game. He knew that she wasn't about to let a game get in the way of dinner time. Their own Mom had started that rule and Janet enforced it strictly with both her own family and with him. There would be no TV trays or standing over the kitchen sink to eat today.

Janet poured each of them a glass of wine and sat down across from him at his kitchen table. She waited for him to take the first bite, then smiled when she saw the delight on his face.

There's something so calming about my Sis. Mark thought. *She takes on life so easily. Why can't I be more like her?*

Despite the fact she had her own family to cook for, she took pleasure in sharing her Sundays with her big brother. He also knew that when she chose to cook in his kitchen instead of having dinner at her house, she often had something on her mind.

"What's up?" he asked. "Or did you just come over to make me the most scrumptious enchiladas *ever.*"

Janet laughed and took a bite, nodding her head in agreement over his assessment of her efforts.

"Not much," she said between bites. "I kinda needed a break from the kiddos though—especially the older one. She's driving me crazy with her all-important years. About to start second grade and you'd think she was already a teenager."

She took a small sip and let the wine sit in her mouth for a moment before swallowing.

"I also needed a break from going through Mom's stuff. Just started tackling the ton of pictures she had in our really living room. Early on, she kept them all neatly labeled in albums. More recently, she just started throwing them into boxes just like with her papers. I got this crazy idea I could sort them all out and make separate albums for Bill, you, and my-self. My crazy idea has resulted in a den that is over-flowing with Mom's old stuff."

"Yeah, but what a great Christmas present that would be for Bill and me," Mark said between bites.

"I guess that was my intention." Her fork came down. "But I thought they'd be better if you added some of your own stuff. Do you have any pictures of you as a baby?"

"I'm not much for taking or collecting pic-tures, Sis."

"Darn. I thought maybe she'd given you your baby pictures. I can't seem to find anything of when you were really little. There were so many of me and plenty of you as a toddler, then as we got older, especially you in your various athletic uniforms. But I'd like to start with the early days."

Mark sat back to think for a minute. Although his mom had plenty of stories of when he was a baby, he really couldn't visualize any specific pictures.

"I know from the stories Mom and Dad had no money when I was born. I've often wondered if maybe I wasn't exactly *planned*. Maybe they didn't have a camera back then or they couldn't afford film or developing. We didn't have cell phones or iPads that recorded our every waking moment digitally like we have now. I'm sure there are pictures somewhere, just not many."

Janet smiled. "Yeah, I guess you could be right. The amount of pictures in her collection seemed to grow exponentially as the years went on."

She patted at the side of her mouth with a napkin, then took a sip of water.

"Of course, as we've always said, you are the odd ball of the family. Maybe you were adopted."

Mark knew his sister was just teasing as she had many times before. But for the first time, it bothered him. Where was his birth certificate? Where were the baby pictures?

CHAPTER TEN

SHE PULLED THE THIN BLANKET up over her head, but it didn't shut off the sounds coming from the next room—the horrible weeping and pleading. The women's anguished, *"Why? Why are you doing this?"* followed by more pleading and weeping. Who did he have in there?

The first time she'd heard the sounds, she'd tried to scream. Somehow, she thought it might stop what was going on. But all it did was bring him to her door, a dark figure looming in the door frame. Her only thought was: am I next?

Yet he hadn't touched her. He hadn't done anything except stand in the doorway panting and staring at her.

This time, she was silent. If her wild screams yielded nothing, this place, this horrible room, must be somewhere where no one could hear.

Yet her silence did no good. As before, when the other woman's pleading ceased, he came to stand in her doorway, peering into the room, his eyes clouded by the darkness.

Oh god, he was crossing the room towards her. Reaching her side with just a few steps. He stood next to her bed, his arms crossed, his back ramrod straight. She struggled with the rope and managed to turn her face and part of her body away from him.

But again, the feared attack did not come. Instead, she felt him sit on the edge of the bed.

"Don't be afraid," he said, his voice now low and steady as if he was trying to soothe her. Her curiosity made her turn her head back, and the expression on his face confused her. His eyes were dreamy, not looking at her at all. He was rubbing his palms down both sides of his face as if trying to get his mind to work right.

He dropped his hands abruptly.

"I know it sounds like I'm hurting her. But it's just adults being adults. You know that. You're old enough for me to tell you this hurts me, too. At least in my heart. I guess I waited too long. I can't seem to make it happen."

What the hell?

His shoulders sagged, and she was shocked to see moisture in his dark eyes.

"I couldn't help it, Darling," he said. "They wouldn't let me go. They just kept getting closer and closer, and I eventually just had to accept it."

His mood shifted quickly again and anger crossed his features.

"I told them again and again how important it was for me to find you. I finally had to play along."

His words only terrified her more. *Who was he talking about? Had he escaped from prison?*

"I intended to find Marjorie first, but there you were—just as I'd imagined. Just as I knew you would be."

He smiled then, reached out his arms and tried to pull her towards him. His black fingernails and the grease ground into his hands made her nauseous.

Was he trying to *hug* her? She fought him then, her fists hindered by the ropes. She slapped and clawed and tried to do some damage. But all it did was set off his temper.

CHAPTER ELEVEN

Monday, November 14

SAM OSBORNE WAS WAITING for Mark at the office Monday morning casually sipping the mud the break room tried to pass off as coffee. Mark was impressed not just by his iron stomach, but his early arrival.

The man must have been up and on the road at three-thirty to get here by eight, he thought. *He also must know a few of my coworkers to have made himself so at home.*

The older detective smiled, and Mark was once again caught up in the warmth that came with it.

"Morning. What thoughts have been going through that head of yours this morning, Detective?" Sam asked.

Mark sat, then swiveled in his chair and read from his computer screen.

"A couple of people on duty yesterday checked out different angles to both women, but so far, they've come up with no connections."

He turned back to Sam.

"We'll keep digging there. In the meantime, I'm headed back to Carla's apartment complex this morning to talk to her roommate Melissa again and maybe a few more neighbors."

"Mind if I tag along 'pardner'?" Sam asked in a badly done John Wayne accent.

"Glad to have you. We can stop at the Starbucks on the way and get you some decent coffee," Mark said.

Mark was once again struck by the bleakness ingrained on Melissa Burns' face—it didn't go with her petite frame or the perkiness of her curls. He could see that her roommate's disappearance had taken its toll over the weekend. Deep shadows circled her eyes, and she looked like she hadn't slept.

"You talked to her mom?" Melissa said. "She hasn't heard anything either? No demands for ransom or anything?" Her voice was unsteady as if she didn't really want an affirmative answer to those questions.

"We don't think money is behind this, Melissa …Ms. Burns." Mark said. "Her family is not well off. But no, no one has contacted her relatives to ask for anything."

Mark introduced Melissa to Sam.

"Carla's mom has hired Sam to help with this investigation. Mind if he also asks some questions?"

Melissa glanced towards Sam, but didn't seem to see him. She ran a palm over her face slowly, stopping at her chin, then refocused on him and nodded her head to finally acknowledge his presence.

"Mark's filled me in on what you told him in that last interview, Ms. Burns," Sam began. "I know Carla didn't have a steady boyfriend, but I was wondering, was there anyone she dated on a regular basis in recent years? Does she have any other women or men she socialized with or hung out with to study besides you?"

Melissa's hand fell to her side.

"As I told Mark, she's pretty much consumed with school right now. She's very close to getting her master's degree."

"So, she didn't date much? Didn't have time for it or just wasn't into men … or women?" Sam asked.

Melissa raised one eyebrow, a gesture Mark had always admired in the few people who could do it. In her, it turned cuteness into intellect.

"She wasn't gay if that's what you're asking. And she had a boyfriend when she moved here. Someone originally from Lancaster like her. He's enrolled at Richmond, but as far as I know, they haven't gone out since the early days of college. I think she stayed in touch, though. She mentioned texting him or talking to him a few times."

"Do you know his name?" Mark asked.

"Matthew … Matthew Olson. He's in the engineering program at Richmond. Finishing up his degree and a T.A. I think. But I never met him, and she never spoke of him like he was a creep or a stalker or anything."

"What about your neighbor Todd Walker," Sam said, referring to his notes. "Did he ever ask her out or act interested in her?"

Melissa's forehead furrowed.

"The guy across the hall? We barely know him. We've seen him in the hallway to say 'hi,' but Carla never mentioned him. If he was interested in her, I didn't know about it."

Mark envisioned the guy staring through his peephole. *Guess he keeps his 'interest' level to voyeurism,* he thought.

"Can you think of anyone else who may have liked her a bit too much or maybe someone she *didn't* get along with? Or do you know of someone she might have been interested in?" Mark asked.

"Carla was nice to everyone," Melissa said. She massaged her temples as if she were developing a headache, but met Mark's eyes as she added, "She didn't have an aggressive bone in her body."

But Mark noticed she didn't say anything about the second half of the question.

The detectives strolled from the parking garage to the engineering building of the University of

Richmond, chatting about their impressions of the other neighbors they'd been able to interview. They agreed they hadn't learned much new, that Carla and Melissa had pretty much kept to themselves.

At the building, Mark stepped forward to hold the door open for Sam, then gazed around them at the campus, admiring the lushness of greenery, the slight rise of the hills, the stately brick buildings, before walking into the building.

The detectives referred to the slip of paper containing Matthew Olson's schedule before finding the right classroom.

They pulled him from Room 242 after apologizing to the professor for interrupting his class and showing the teacher the note of explanation from the Administration Office.

Matthew stood outside with them, glancing up and down the empty hallway, as if being interviewed was embarrassing and he was hoping to finish before class let out.

"I mean it's awful what you're saying, that she's gone missing and all," he said. "But I haven't seen her in a while. I mean we haven't dated in a long time," he said.

"So the last time you spoke to her was …?" Sam prodded.

"Two-three weeks maybe? Although we got caught up a few times on text."

"And she seemed fine when you talked and chatted by text?" Sam added.

Matthew ran one hand over his mouth and finally set his gaze on the detectives. He looked from one to the other, judging where to present his next remark. He settled on Sam.

"I know this is gonna sound weird, but last week she seemed kinda excited about something. It was just a text, but she said she'd gotten some news and wanted to talk to me about it—she was trying to figure out what to do about it, and wanted to know if I'd listen."

"Did you two get together then?" Mark asked.

Matthew turned towards Mark.

"I told her to call instead. I have a new girlfriend. I didn't think the new boo would appreciate me going out somewhere with the old one, even if it's been forever since Carla and I dated."

Matthew crossed his arms lowered his gaze to his own feet, giving himself a moment to think. He sighed and uncrossed his arms like he'd made up his mind.

"Carla didn't have that many friends besides that roommate of hers. I think she kept in touch because she needed someone else to talk to once in a while. I suspect she may have still liked me, but I assure you, the feeling wasn't mutual."

He glanced down the hall again, then addressed Mark.

"I don't mean to sound conceited or anything, but … Look, Carla can be a little needy sometimes. She wanted to get together, but I put her off. I guess

I wasn't ready to deal with whatever drama she had going on. It wasn't really my business, and I don't know why she wanted to meet in person. It made me realize the next time I saw her I needed to tell her about the new girlfriend. But she never even called."

Mark referred to his notebook.

"Does the name Alice Springer mean anything to you?"

"Sounds like a pretty common name. But I don't think so. Should I know her?"

"And Carla gave no indication of what she was excited about? Something about school or her personal life or dating?" Mark said.

Matthew gave the question a moment as if reaching into his memory.

But he shook his head.

"Nope. I don't think it had anything to do with a guy. I don't think she'd bring that up. That's why I thought it was weird she was telling me about it. I guess it could have been something about school or getting her master's. She only said something about discovering she wasn't who she thought she was."

Sam and Mark said their goodbyes and walked out together.

"Well?" Sam asked Mark.

"I don't think he had anything to do with it, but that's just my gut. I'll have the office check out where he was the night Carla was taken, and affirm he has a new girlfriend. I also think we have to find out more about this daddy issue. It sounds like it could be the news she wanted to share with her old beau."

His phone rang. Mark looked at the number and then stopped outside the car to answer. A few un-huhs later, he disconnected and put the phone back in his pocket.

Sam could see that whatever Mark had learned was significant. He had that hungry detective look on his face that was part puzzle/part yearning to push further.

They settled in their seats and Mark put the key in the ignition, but before he cranked up the engine, he turned to Sam.

"That was the chief. There's been another missing person's case. That's three in just over a week. This one doesn't sound related to Carla either but …"

"You don't believe in coincidences," Sam finished.

Mark and Sam sat in Captain McCoy's office.

"Kinda like old times, huh Sam?" Bob McCoy said.

Sam smiled at his old friend.

"Except you're running things, the FBI is about to become involved and you live in another city so we can't have Mabel's coffee and maple-glazed donuts while we talk," Sam said. Sam was referring to the place in Lancaster where the two of them often met for a chat in the years Bob was on the force there and Sam was a private investigator. They'd been together on the Philadelphia police force in their early years, young cops hungry to battle the evils of the world. *We've done a lot of that together over the years,* Sam thought.

Bob grimaced at the coffee he was drinking.

"No, not exactly Mabel's, that's for sure. It's good to have you here with us," Bob said. "We can use the help, even with FBI on the way. Because of the timing of the disappearances, we've set up a task force. Mark's on the force, of course, and FBI Agent Pete Juarez will be part of it. But you know how I feel about the feds. I trust your instincts as much as their abundant resources."

He put his glasses back on and picked up a sheet of paper from his desk.

"I found out about this third case from another old friend of mine—the sheriff near the Charlottesville, Virginia area. He saw our missing persons reports go out and called me this morning. They put out an alert at about ten a.m. about a missing seventy-two-year-old woman in his area, and he wanted to make sure I saw it."

"A silver alert?" Mark asked.

"Silver alerts go out for someone who has wandered off because of Dementia. I don't think that's the case here, though the fact she's in a wheelchair and on several medications means she's a high alert case. This woman disappeared yesterday afternoon after meeting up with a funeral director … at least that's where the woman said she was going."

"There's some doubt?" Sam asked.

"They couldn't track down the director."

Bob adjusted his glasses and referred to the report.

"It says here that Helen Tompkins was reported missing by her daughter, Millie Perkins on Sunday, November thirteen when she failed to return home after an appointment with an unknown funeral director. No contact info was left for the director, no mention of which funeral home she intended to make arrangements with. The daughter's primary concern is that her mother is diabetic and needs her glipizide as well as several other medications. Helen Tompkins is described by her daughter as extremely independent, despite confinement to a wheelchair, and is not characteristically prone to disappearing for periods of time."

Bob put down the piece of paper he was reading and took off his glasses to rub his eyes.

"Three people in a week," Mark said. "A twenty-two-year-old student, a forty-five-year old housewife and a seventy-two-year-old woman in a wheelchair."

Bob rested one hand on top of the report, a gesture Sam recognized meant he was ready to render an opinion.

"A connection doesn't make a lot of sense as is, but we have to keep an open mind. Juarez will be here this afternoon to start with the Carla Dunlap thing, and the agency may be able to help all of us connect the dots, if there are any dots to connect. I want you two to continue your pursuit in cooperation—Mark's lead on the case and can coordinate the task force. We don't have jurisdiction in Lancaster, Winchester, or Charlottesville, but since Sam is a private eye, he's working on this independently. The law enforcement agencies have all been alerted and are willing to work with us. Sam, I hope you can stick around to help Mark?"

"As long as it takes," Sam said.

On the way back to Mark's office, the younger detective turned to Sam.

"I have a big old house and I owe you the hospitality. You're welcome to stay with me if you want."

Sam smiled at the young detective. He was beginning to appreciate how comfortable the two were together. It had been a long time since he'd worked with a partner.

CHAPTER TWELVE

"THE REPORT SAYS Helen Tompkins' daughter, Millie Perkins, last talked to her on Saturday," Mark read from the computer in his office.

Sam sat across from him nibbling on a stale donut he'd snatched from the lunchroom. They hadn't had time to grab lunch before heading back to the office. *Definitely not Mabel's*, he thought, before wrapping it into his napkin and tossing it into the trash.

"Millie was supposed to bring her mother an evening meal Sunday. She reports having called to confirm early in the afternoon, but no one answered the phone," Mark continued. "The caregiver, a Mrs. Rebecca Weeks, does not answer the Tompkins phone."

"Millie Tompkins said she went to the house and ran into the caregiver, who reminded her that Helen had scheduled a talk with a funeral director. Millie then returned home. The caregiver left at the usual time of five p.m. and Millie says her mother still wasn't answering the phone at six-thirty p.m. Millie then drove to Helen's home and says the casserole she'd brought earlier remained in the fridge."

Sam picked up a pen from the front of Mark's desk and began clicking it.

"She called the police and filed a report an hour later," Mark said.

"Anyone see anything?" Sam said. He stared at the pen and stopped clicking, realizing it was a nervous gesture.

"Neighbors were canvassed at that time, and one of them reported seeing Helen Tompkins being helped into a light-colored mini-van by a man—no struggle," he continued. "The description of the man, however, is completely vague—average height, average build. The witness couldn't come up with hair color or even tell whether the person was Caucasian or another nationality."

"If this is all somehow connected, this perp is not taking people randomly," Sam said, rubbing his chin. "He's planned for this. Helen Tompkins went willingly, so she must have been convinced she was in no danger. The other two also seemed to have disappeared without any commotion."

Mark also started rubbing his chin, and Sam could see his mind was whirring as fast as his own.

"What, Mark? What are you thinking?"

Mark's hand dropped to the desktop with a thud.

"I just got off the phone with our audio/video department five minutes ago. Although the grocery store where Alice Springer disappeared didn't have a functioning camera, the store across the street handed in their tape. It's too far away to show much, but it does show Alice chatting it up with a guy who was apparently parked close to her. She got into his car at one point, then the rain started coming down so hard, the images aren't clear."

He began absently rubbing the desk top.

"Then there's Carla's situation. If whoever is responsible for her disappearance has something to do with her finding out about her possible birth fathers, the perp has to either be connected to the family or have come across the information somehow. I think I should talk to Melissa again. See if she can give us a better lead in that direction. And let's go talk to June Grindage, the mechanic's sister."

He used both palms to push himself to standing.

Sam stood as well and picked up the paper file Bob had run off for him.

"Think we might get some lunch on the way?"

June Grindage lived in a walk-up unit over several small stores in the Carytown neighborhood of Richmond. The neighborhood was known for its art galleries and restaurants. June's apartment was situated over the gallery she ran.

The detectives stopped for a quick bite at a trendy coffee shop painted pink and purple and situated across the street from the brick, two-level building that contained June's gallery and home.

"Thank you, gentlemen, for agreeing to meet me here," June said at her door. "I'm trying to finish getting ready for a showing tonight. I've got a couple hours, but we've still got a lot to do."

She gestured to her couch, and once the detectives were situated, picked up the pot of coffee resting on a table along with three mugs.

"Would you like some cookies? I made them myself—baking is kind of my stress reliever and this showing has me running."

Sam smiled. June's long flowered skirt and peasant blouse fit the image of an artist while the fact coffee mugs were already on the table showed she was an organized business woman.

"We appreciate the coffee, and we don't need much of your time," Sam said. "And I would *never* say 'no' to a homemade cookie," he said.

Her skirt flowed with her as she crossed over to the kitchen area and transferred several cookies from a tin on the counter to a china plate. Sam used the moment to study the apartment. It was an odd mix of atmospheres that somehow went together: splashes of bright color, but a beige sofa, statuettes placed on the few available flat spaces, a handful of paintings on the wall. Sam admired her taste, but wondered how someone could live in such a tiny place. He supposed she spent a lot of time down in her gallery.

When June was settled in her chair, Mark began the questioning.

"We know you're friends with Katherine Dunlap. We've assumed that by agreeing to meet with us, you know what's happened."

June's hostess smile vanished. All she said was, "Of course."

"Katherine also told us that you've kept in touch with Carla. That since she moved to Richmond to attend the university, she and you have gotten together a few times."

"A few," was all June offered.

Sam jumped into the conversation, trying to turn it toward the more personal.

"Katherine hired me to investigate, Miss Grindage. I know that she'd want you to tell us if you know anything—even if it means telling us stuff she doesn't know herself that might help her daughter."

June was not looking at either of her visitors. She sat stiff-backed in the winged chair she'd chosen and ran one finger around the rim of her mug.

"Actually, Carla and I had grown fairly close. We didn't see each other often, but she'd come here to this area when she needed a break from university, and we'd have dinner together."

"And the last time you did that?" Mark asked.

June's eyes came up from her mug and focused on Mark.

"About two weeks ago. She said school was driving her crazy, and asked if we could spend a day gallery diving and go to a favorite restaurant of hers: the Crazy Cow.

"Gallery diving?" Mark asked.

She smiled into her mug.

"Sorry. It's a term we made up. We get all dressed up in our most artsy clothes and visit studios and act like we are serious buyers. Neither one of us could afford most of the pieces, of course. But she loves art as much as I do."

Sam could see the affection this woman had for Carla, but he also sensed her worry. Her eyes glanced out the window as if searching for the missing girl.

"It was really just a distraction, a way to get out of our everyday lives and dress up to forget our worries."

"And when you got together for this latest visit, did she seem upset about anything in particular or talk to you about what was going on," Sam asked.

"No, not really."

Something about her tone made Sam doubt that she was telling the truth. She wasn't looking out the window anymore but she didn't meet his eyes either. She'd resumed circling the mug rim.

"So she didn't mention anything she'd found out recently that might have upset her?" he prodded.

Her gaze came up from the cup, and Sam saw genuine confusion.

"She didn't mention her father?" he asked.

"Why would she mention her father?" June asked. "He passed away a year ago."

Sam and Mark exchanged glances. Unless she was lying, she didn't know about what Carla had found out.

"Did she happen to mention her old boyfriend Matthew Olson? Do you know if she still had feelings for Matthew?" Sam asked.

June's eyebrows went up.

"Matthew was ancient history, Mr. Osborne. I know for a fact she had no lingering desire to pursue him in any other way."

"So, she specifically said that … she was over him and had moved on?"

"Well, no. But she never talked about him at all. I think if she felt that way, it would have come up."

"Did she talk about any other guys she was involved with or anyone that made her uncomfortable? A neighbor perhaps?"

June shook her head.

"She didn't talk about any neighbors, and she was not dating anyone," June said. But the note of finality in her tone gave Sam pause. *She knew something she wasn't sharing.*

Back at the Richmond police headquarters, Mark stood at his desk and stretched out his shoulder muscles.

"Okay Sam. Let's see if we can find you somewhere to work. We had a man transferred last week so I think maybe we have an extra cubby."

The two walked out of Mark's office into the inner circle of desks, lost in their thoughts. Mark pointed to an empty desk and reached across to turn on the computer screen.

"Let's go over our notes. Maybe we'll see something we've missed. I know you said you had some calls to make. I'll run back to Melissa's, talk to her, then come and collect you about five or five-thirty. We'll have a beer before we head over to my place. That is … if it's all right with you."

"Sure," Sam said, already engrossed in his notes and the computer. He looked up briefly as Mark left.

Three times talking to Melissa, he thought. *Wonder why he didn't just call.*

CHAPTER THIRTEEN

WHAT SAM DIDN'T KNOW was that Mark was asking himself the same question. He was drawn to this witness, and he wasn't sure why. He couldn't seem to get her red hair and bright blue eyes out of his mind. He kept envisioning the desperate look in those eyes. Despite her openness and her confession about the father issue, he also suspected she was holding something back.

He felt a pull towards this woman that had nothing to do with the case.

Mark pulled up in front of the apartment complex and called from his car.

"Miss Burns?"

"Yes?"

"This is Mark Brady. I wondered if you had a few minutes for coffee. I'm in the neighborhood and …"

"Oh, sure. I'm in between classes and don't have another until seven tonight. Do you know the Java Hut on Ninth?"

Mark agreed to meet her in ten minutes and wondered why she hadn't ask what this was about. *Did she think he was asking her out? Did it matter? Did he wish he* was *asking her out?*

Melissa eyes were finally free of puffiness, though the fear was still there. She smiled warmly, however, when she spotted him already seated with a steaming latte.

He stood as she arrived at the table, then settled back down as she went to place an order. He'd had enough caffeine for one day, but he'd ordered a decaf just to have something to hold. She came back and sat with a giant muffin and a tea in front of her. Mark watched as she concentrated on the tea cup, her delicate fingers restlessly pushing the tea bag to steep before she spoke, then tearing little chunks of the muffin off and popping them into her mouth.

"My diet has gone to hell in the last week," she said.

"That's understandable," he said.

Her eyes came up from the tea bag and muffin to connect with his, and he sensed her relax: the deep blue of her irises actually seemed to lighten; the lines around her mouth smoothed. He felt like she was an old friend he'd known for a long time who was stopping by for a chat. Did she feel it, too?

Shaking himself inwardly, he set down his coffee cup and began.

"Thank you for seeing me again," he said. "I'm glad you suggested this place. The stuff they serve at headquarters is disgusting. I needed a good brew."

She smiled and continued dunking her tea bag.

She must like really strong tea, he thought. *Why doesn't that surprise me? And why oh why do I find that simple little gesture charming?*

He straightened in his chair, determined to rid himself of the distracting little thoughts that seemed to creep into his head when she was around.

"I wanted to see if you had any insight at all as to how word may have got out about Carla having a possible birth father that wasn't Charles. I think it may be the key in all this."

She didn't say anything so he continued.

"We talked to Mrs. Dunlap and she says she never told Carla. That, in fact, very few people even knew about it. We talked to June Grindage here in Richmond, and I don't think Carla confided in her about it either."

"I already told you. Carla overheard her mom telling her sister," Melissa said.

"And that explains how she found out, but not how someone else might know. We think this 'Dad' in the note may have been a ruse to get her to meet at McDonalds at the designated time."

Melissa eyes rounded.

"Of course. That makes sense."

Suddenly she glanced around her at the neighboring tables. At this time of day, they were mostly empty.

Her gaze returned to his, and he saw realization hit. Her hands grasped the sides of the table.

"Oh, god. Of course."

"Of course?" he asked.

"She broke the news to me in a coffee shop. It wasn't this one—it was the one where students hang out on Thirteenth Street. But it was packed as usual, and she was upset. She poured it all out to me. Someone could have overheard." Her hands came up to her cheeks and her eyes filled.

Mark couldn't help himself. He reached across the table and put a steadying hand on her forearm. Something about this girl made him want to carry around a protective shield to deflect all the woes that were pounding her down.

"That's okay. You remembered. That's good. It gives us something to go on—something to look into."

But despite his calm tone, soothing words and his touch, her face remained frozen, the worry lines framing her eyes and her lips.

"There's something else," she said.

He didn't say anything, realizing his hunch about her holding back was about to prove itself true. She wanted to share.

"I've gone back and forth in my head about saying something about this, but I can't keep it inside. I'm sorry. I'm really sorry."

"Sorry? What on earth do you have to be sorry for?" Mark asked softly.

She still hadn't picked up her tea, but she finally took the bag out and laid it on a napkin. With another napkin, she dabbed at her eyes, trying to gain control over her emotions.

"I promised Carla I would never tell anyone. I found out just a week or so before she disappeared. But I swore I wouldn't say anything to anyone. She was so afraid it would get back to her mother."

"What is it, Melissa?" Mark said, keeping his voice soft and nonthreatening. When she didn't respond right away, he added: "You obviously know something that you think is important. I promise I'll do what I can not to hurt her with this information, but it's more important to protect her now."

Melissa used two fingers to massage her forehead. The fingers went to her hair and twirled a few curls. Finally, she looked him in the face and he saw it there: trust. She believed he'd keep his word.

"Carla did have a boyfriend—a man friend anyway—a lover maybe. I'm not sure I'd call him a boyfriend exactly. He was twelve years older than her, and they kept it a secret. They didn't even really date."

"Why?" Mark asked. But he was pretty sure he already knew the answer. The pretty co-ed. The lonely student. The older man who gave her the attention she craved. He'd seen it too many times.

"He's married."

"That's not good," Mark said.

"Oh, that's only the beginning. He's also a minister … with two kids."

Mark sighed. Sometimes he hated being right.

"But they were in love," he said, not even pretending it was a question.

Two fat tears finally escaped her tired eyes and trailed down her face.

"I know. It sounds horrible. But I've never seen her so happy. So assured. So glad to be alive. It hadn't been going on long—a couple of months. I think she told me because she was carrying around this huge burden of guilt about his family."

"And she needed to unload … and you were the vehicle," Mark said.

"She said it was instant attraction. She said he was going to leave his wife, his children and his church—he was that much in love with her."

Mark said nothing. Was Melissa one of those people that others felt comfortable telling their secrets to, then asking her to "never breathe a word to a soul." Was that why she'd gone into psychology? Still, he found it hard to believe that this intelligent woman sitting across from him had fallen for Carla's fairy tale love story.

As though she could sense what he was thinking, Melissa cut in. "I know it sounds stupid. I know she was probably kidding herself. I also know what a fool I was to keep it from the police. It's why I'm glad you called."

She took a sip of her tea as if to steady herself, then slumped back in her chair, shaking her head like she couldn't believe how stupid she'd been.

Melissa sat up straighter, picked up the mug and studied its contents, but Mark knew it was an avoidance mechanism.

"I need a name, Melissa," he said. "You know I do."

Without looking up, she whispered, "Joe Williams…United Methodist Church in York."

Again, Mark couldn't help himself. He laid a gentle hand on her wrist. She stared first at his hand, then brought her eyes up to meet his.

"This will break Mrs. Dunlap's heart," she said. "And that woman has enough to deal with. How can we give her more pain?"

"Sometimes pain is necessary to get to the truth," Mark said. He patted her wrist once before sitting back and taking out his notebook to write down the name.

"But we have to investigate this and there's no way we can keep it from Mrs. Dunlap."

He looked up before adding, "However, if he had anything at all to do with this …"

He saw the flame ignite in Melissa's eyes.

"I'll kill him myself," she said.

CHAPTER FOURTEEN

Tuesday, November 15

SAM AND MARK DROVE to Winchester separately this time—Sam on his way home, Mark to ask some follow ups now that there were three cases and a few more suspects.

George Springer greeted them at the door, hope blooming on his face. "Do you have news? Has something happened?"

"I'm afraid not, Mr. Springer. We just have a couple of follow up questions," Mark said. "Can we talk to both of you for just a few minutes."

"Why not?" George said. He seemed to have lost some of his combativeness, but gained a heavy load of weariness. Another few days had left him a little more defeated. George lead them to the living room, then called for Mary.

Before any questions came up, George started talking, but he wasn't really addressing anyone.

"I don't understand. Alice is only a housewife. I know she didn't just skip town on a whim. Where could she be? Who would take her away from us?"

Mary sat, but didn't even try to comfort her rambling father this time.

"Do you think there's a chance she's still with us?" she asked, her voice almost a whisper.

Mark heard George gasp at the remark. Had they not discussed the possibility?

Mark cleared his throat, which got both the rambling George and the frightened Mary's attention.

"I wanted to ask about Alice's car," Mark said. "Has she had any other mechanical trouble with it lately?"

Father and daughter exchanged a look as if to ask: *what does this have to do with anything?*

George turned back to address the detective. "I kept the car in great shape for her. I always made sure it was serviced. It was an older car, but it never left her abandoned and it certainly didn't just loosen its own battery cable!"

"We know that Mr. Springer. I was just wondering if she'd had any trouble with it recently, maybe …?"

Mary interrupted his comment.

"Just last week."

All three men turned toward her.

"She called me and said she might need a ride. She didn't want to wait for Triple-A to show. Why didn't I think of that?" She pushed against her forehead with her palm.

"Was it the same grocery store?" Sam asked.

Mary shook her head. "No. No, it wasn't that store. It was a coffee shop not far from here. Just a couple of blocks away."

"Did you pick her up then?" Mark asked as he scribbled notes.

When she didn't reply right away, he glanced up from his notebook to see her face paler, her eyes gone wide.

"No. I didn't need to. She called back a few minutes later. Some stranger looked under the hood and said it a simple problem. He fixed the car and she was on her way. She kept going on about how nice he was when she got home."

Mary leaned forward in her seat and her arms went around her waist.

"Oh god. That was him, wasn't it!"

Mark returned to his notes. "If you could give us the name of the coffee shop and address, we'll follow up."

He looked up at Mary.

"The grocery store's security cameras weren't operational, and no one at the store saw her actually get into another car. But a camera across from the store shows her chatting with the man parked next to her and then getting into what was probably his vehicle. Would your mom get into a car with someone she didn't know?"

"No, I don't think she would. She had to have known him, didn't she!" Mary said.

"The son-of-a-bitch tampered with her car—*twice*," George said between clenched teeth.

"The camera didn't show that from the angle we could see and it was raining hard so our view of the whole thing was somewhat obstructed. We did see him pull up next to her *after* she arrived and go into the store. And, we think the rain may have contributed to her getting into his car later," Mark said.

The room grew silent for a moment as the Springers absorbed this information. Mark looked over at Sam and gave a slight nod, passing the baton.

"Have either of you noticed anyone watching the house in the last few weeks?" Sam asked. "Maybe a car that you don't know parked at the curb?"

Both Springers shook their heads.

"Do either of you know a Carla Dunlap from Richmond?" Sam asked.

George's face now matched his daughter's in paleness, and his voice was shaky as he asked: "Isn't that the girl on the news? The student who's gone missing? My god. Is it the same guy?"

"It's not likely, but we are not ruling it out," Mark said quickly.

"How about a Reverend Joe Williams?" Sam asked. "Have you heard that name?"

The Springers shook their heads.

"He's the pastor at York United Methodist in Pennsylvania?" Mark added.

Mary tilted her head to one side.

"Wait, yeah. I think I *have* heard about him. I've heard he's really good, but I don't know why I know that."

George's already pale face now looked shell shocked as he turned to his daughter.

"Probably because your mom and Betty went there recently." He turned back to the detectives.

"Betty's folks are from York, and she'd been attending that church when she could get over there on Sunday to see her folks. She's Methodist. I didn't know the preacher's name, but both Betty and Alice raved about his sermons and talked about his radio program."

He kneaded his cheeks as if trying to get the color back, then clasp his hands together as he added: "My wife came home and declared that she'd finally found a decent preacher and joked about moving to York!"

The detectives went next to the home of Betty Farthing. Betty was a childhood friend of Alice Springer and a frequent companion to church services, which George would not attend.

News of Alice's disappearance must have hit the airwaves sometime in the last twenty-four hours if Betty's distraught expression was any indication. She wrung her hands and started talking the moment she found out they were law enforcement.

"This is terrible. Horrible. Why would someone harm Alice? She was just the nicest. I've known her since middle school. We don't see each other often, but … I can't believe this has happened to my *friend*!"

Betty was still standing at her front door.

"We don't know yet if this is a kidnapping, but we're looking into all the possibilities," Mark said.

"What else could it be?" Betty asked. Realizing they were still outside, she'd motioned the detectives in.

"We're just trying to check all angles. We wanted to ask you a couple of things about Alice and her recent mood and how you two know each other," Mark said. He gingerly maneuvered around a table completely filled with cat figurines to follow her to a seating area. The woman was a collector, if evidenced by the various cats, dogs and bears that crammed every available shelf.

"I'm not sure how I can help. I haven't seen Alice in … oh, let me see. I guess the last time was went we went to church together in Pennsylvania a couple weeks ago," Betty said as she plunked her ample seat down into a chair.

Mark sat on the couch and opened his notebook. Sam sat next to him.

"Would that be York United Methodist?" Mark asked.

Betty's mouth dropped open.

"How did you know that?"

"George Springer mentioned it. We asked if he knew Reverend Joe Williams, and he said you and Alice had gone to his church and liked his sermon. Is that correct?"

Her eyebrows drew together.

"What does Reverend Joe have to do with Alice going missing?"

"Our connection with his church and the reverend isn't something we can share at this point. We're checking this out in relation to both Alice and another matter. What was your impression of the man?"

Betty's concern over her friend was suddenly replaced by a flash of temper. She blinked hard and her lips drew together. Then she leaned back against the cushion of her chair and crossed her arms.

"Are you trying to insinuate Reverend Joe is involved somehow? If so, you're way off base. He's a very good man with an important message to tell the world. He certainly wouldn't have run off with Alice on a whim, nor would Alice do such a thing."

Mark just looked up from his notebook, a puzzled expression on his face. Sam put his hands up, palms towards Betty.

"We don't mean anything of the sort, Mrs. Farthing," he said. "Please, we're just checking out some issues."

Both men watched closely as Betty calmed herself by taking a deep breath. She smoothed her hands down across her knees.

"Oh, okay. Well we both very much liked what he had to say. I've been back several times and Alice said she'd be going with me this Sunday again."

Her expression crumbled as she added, "Guess that's not going to happen."

CHAPTER FIFTEEN

BEFORE HE HEADED HOME to Maggie in Lancaster, Sam had one stop. He needed to talk to Katherine Dunlap. He called Maggie from the road to tell her he'd be home soon, then pulled up to the Dunlap home.

The expression on Katherine's face as she opened the door was the same one that greeted Sam and Mark at the Springer home. Was there news? Had her daughter just been partying somewhere with a friend? Sam felt that look in his gut and remembered how horrible the aftershock of reality in a situation like this was. How many times had hope about Davie been dashed by someone at the door?

"No. I'm sorry, Katherine," he said. "I don't have any news. Just a few more questions. Mind if I come in?"

He hated watching Katherine's expression fall and anxiety creep back into her eyes. She waved him in and asked if he wanted coffee.

"Thanks, but no thanks. I'm on my way home and needed to check in and talk about some things."

Katherine settled across from him.

"You said you had questions?"

"You told me Carla didn't have a boyfriend that you knew of. Is that correct?" Sam asked. He glanced over to see her nodding her head.

"That's right. I mean she never mentioned one. She barely had time to get her school work done—she was on a fast track to get her masters."

"Have you ever heard of a Joe Williams?" He watched her expression closely, trying to see if the words had any effect.

"Do you mean Reverend Joe Williams from York?" she asked, but her expression remained neutral. *She doesn't know,* Sam thought.

"Yes… Reverend Joe Williams from the United Methodist church," he said.

"I know who he is. Carla and I visited his church several times a couple of months ago when our own church was deciding on a new pastor. We didn't care much for the elder who took over the pulpit temporarily at our church and someone had spoken highly of Reverend Williams. I think he has a radio show."

She folded her hands and sat back in her chair.

"I must say—their assessment was right, and I understand how he came to have a show. He's quite a dynamic speaker."

Feeling unsure about how best to approach the next question, Sam rose from his seat and walked over to the window. He gazed out for a few moments before turning back to Katherine.

"What is it, Sam?"

"I've been told that Carla and the reverend were involved."

Katherine jumped to her feet, her face twisted in shock and anger. "That's ridiculous. Who would say such a thing? He's a married man. Carla would never do that!"

Sam patted down the air in front of him, trying to calm her down.

"I'm sorry to tell you that. But the source I have is reliable."

She stood shaking her head.

"No. That's not right. As far as I know, Carla never went back to that church. I don't know who you've talk to but …"

"Katherine. I'm pretty sure there was something going on. This isn't gossip. The person who told us this didn't want to say anything about it, but her conscience wouldn't permit her to keep it quiet."

As suddenly as she'd jumped up, Katherine fell back onto her seat, her face pale, her eyes wide open.

"I can't believe that. I *don't* believe it. There's been a mistake. Your informant is lying."

Sam came to her then, sat down across from her and took her hand.

"Then you didn't know anything about this?"

"I'm sure there's nothing to *know*." But despite the coolness in her tone and the fact she withdrew her hand, Sam didn't think she believed what she said. He needed to let her absorb this piece of news. Sam rose to go.

"Look, Katherine. I'm sorry if I've upset you, but I wouldn't have brought it up if I didn't think it was important. You need to know all the avenues I'm pursuing and this is one of them. My source is reliable, but I'll let you know if I find out anything more about it. I promise."

Back in his car, Sam gave himself a minute. He hated that he'd been put in the position he knew the cops in Davies' case had been in many times: telling a parent that things didn't look so good.

At least it wasn't the ultimate: that Carla's body has been found. Sam was determined to work on the premise that she was alive somewhere, and he'd continue in that vein until he found her.

He placed a call on his cell and put the phone back on its docking station. He started the car and aimed it towards home.

"Danny?" Sam said to the windshield. He pictured the young policeman, who, along with his wife and their two children, had become like family to him.

"Sam? Glad you called. The wife's been bugging me … forgot to ask earlier if you're coming to dinner Sunday."

"I'm not sure. I know it's on the calendar but I'm embroiled in this case. I may be out of town."

"No problem. Just let us know. I will warn you, however, that if you have to miss it, you'll miss Sara's pot roast." Sara and her husband Joseph were part of Danny and Casey's family – former domestic help for Casey's family who now lived with the couple and were godparents to their two children. Dinners on the third Sunday of each month had become a tradition in the Jones home. The memory of Sara's pot roast made Sam's mouth water, and he swiped it with one hand.

"Way to put the pressure on, Danny. We'll see how the week goes. Did you get my text about Joe Williams?"

"Yeah. I've done some calling around. Reverend Williams seems to be very well liked in his community as well as some nearby towns," Danny reported. "He's apparently quite a charismatic speaker and is building a reputation for himself. He already has a radio show and there's talk of a television show."

"And his reputation with the ladies?"

"As far as I can tell, he isn't known for running around on his wife. Everyone I talked to insisted his sermons are down to earth, and that he was a good man who wouldn't cheat on his wife. In fact, several people were quite insulted when I brought it up."

Sam visualized Betty Farthing. He wondered why people were so defensive about the reverend.

"Did anyone in the congregation know Carla Dunlap?"

"Several knew who she was. But only one person went into detail. And what she said wasn't positive. She said Carla hung around the preacher at church events and that she thought Carla had a crush on the man—she idolized him. Do you suppose Carla made more of their relationship than what really existed?"

"It's possible of course. But he also wouldn't be the first man of the cloth to fall from grace with an adoring fan," Sam said. "Thanks for checking around Danny. My love to Casey and the kids."

Sam was tired and glad to be headed back to Lancaster. Talking to Joe Williams would have to wait until tomorrow. Sam needed Maggie and his own home. It was hard to believe they'd been married—he'd been Jenna's father—only a few years. It seemed like he'd known them forever. Maggie was his lifeblood now, and he was anxious to talk to her about this case and his impressions. He was even more anxious just to wrap his weary arms around her. He also wished Jenna wasn't off for her month with Maggie's ex. He could use a child's giggles.

An hour later, he got a passionate kiss at his door and a big plate of spaghetti and meatballs in the kitchen. He then followed Maggie into the living room for tea—their nightly ritual. They hadn't needed to talk at dinner, just recharge their batteries. Now, Sam asked Maggie about her day, anxious to leave the case behind for a few minutes.

Maggie had much to tell. She'd showed a house, closed on another, and had a letter from their daughter Jenna. The little girl's letter was filled with excitement about the zoo, a baseball game and riding on the subway.

By the time Maggie asked Sam about his case, he was too tired to go into much detail. He sketched out a few facts, then asked her if she knew of the preacher.

"The Reverend Joe Williams in York? The one with the radio show?"

Of course, Maggie knew who he meant. He smiled to himself. *How did she do it?* She always seemed to keep up with what was happening in their community—part of her real estate training he guessed.

"That's the one. Her roommate insists Carla Dunlap was having an affair with him."

"Oh, no. I hope that's not the case," she said. She touched her temple with one hand.

"I know he's quite respected. You think we have another community leader fallen? Do you suspect he's involved somehow in her disappearance?"

Sam shrugged.

"We don't know much yet, though we know where he was on the afternoon she disappeared, and it was nowhere near the University of Richmond. But I'm going to talk to him tomorrow before I head back to Richmond."

Sam let out a huge yawn, which triggered a reaction in his wife. She rose from her easy chair, took both their tea cups into the kitchen, then returned to the living room to tell Sam to come to bed. He was snoring softly in his easy chair so she kissed his forehead, covered him with a throw and climbed the steps to their room.

The dream was different this time. The small boy wasn't lost or wandering or running away like in Sam's other dreams. He was just out of Sam's reach. Sam wasn't even sure if this time, the little boy was his son Davie.

The boy was asleep and in the arms of a man whose face Sam couldn't see. The man carrying the boy was standing outside a large car, swearing. He dropped the boy on the grass beside the car and began searching through his pockets.

"Where the hell did I put my keys?" The man glanced around him, as if he shouldn't have spoken aloud. Seeing no one, he turned back to the boy and rolled the small body over, looking underneath. Nothing was there. He stood and leaned his frame against the car door. The latch clicked, startling the

man. He pulled the door open and began searching the front seat, the floor, the dash. His eyes lit on the steering wheel. "Of all the dumb things!" He took the keys from the ignition and went back to the boy, lifting him over a shoulder like a sack of potatoes, walking back to the trunk and unlocking it.

He tossed the small body into the trunk and slammed it shut. Getting into the driver's seat, he inserted the key back into the ignition, started the car and drove away.

Inside the trunk, the boy opened his eyes. He hadn't really been sleeping. "Where am I? What's happening?" No one answered him.

The boy began to cry.

Sam woke up, his body slick with sweat, his hands shaking. He was twisted into the throw and had to free one arm to stand.

He'd been having dreams of losing his son for twenty-five years, and while they'd lessened in intensity, they still came, especially when he got anywhere near a case that involved a kid. This one, while it didn't involve a child, was about people disappearing and the terror it left behind for the families.

The case was taking its toll, but he didn't care. He hadn't been able to get back his son; he might be able to help uncover what had happened to the women.

He turned toward the stairs. He needed to spend the rest of this night in Maggie's warm embrace.

CHAPTER SIXTEEN

THE STAIN ON THE CEILING was beginning to seem familiar. God knows she'd studied it enough. It was that hour in the day he locked them all in their rooms and she heard the terrible sounds of the woman crying.

That poor poor woman. She'd tried talking to the woman the few times they were in the common room.

"Are you all right? Can I do anything for you?"

She'd been met with a vacant stare and a sharp *"silence"* from their captor.

How long had they been here? She wasn't sure. She couldn't remember much of the first few days—her repeated attempts to get away. His quick flashing anger and the binds he never let her out of. She'd almost had the rope loose once—hours spent using her teeth only to have him discover her progress. It was the maddest she'd ever seen him, and she still felt the pain of the ropes as he tightened them even more, then slapped her face.

The sounds from the other room died down and she shivered. Heavy footsteps and the creek of the door alerted her to his arrival, but she didn't look up. She didn't want to see the crazy eyes. She didn't want to smell his horrible breath that often stank of beer.

"I need you to feed Maw Maw again," he said from the doorway, his voice even.

Maw Maw? He wasn't talking about the woman in the other room. He called that woman "honey" and "dear" and fawned over her when they were in the common room—cutting her food and fetching a blanket to tuck around her. He must be talking about the old woman—the woman who sat stonily in the chair, staring straight ahead.

"You know she's a picky eater, but you've always had a way with her. I know you can get her to eat again."

What the hell did he mean—always? She'd fed her once. After watching the elderly woman's nearly catatonic stare, she'd taken up a spoon and tried to help, but the woman had only nibbled a few bites.

Why did he make it sound like she knew the woman? She'd never seen her before the last few days.

How did we all end up in this place?

CHAPTER SEVENTEEN

Wednesday, November 16

THE REVEREND JOE Williams answered his own office door, which opened to the outside of the church. He greeted Sam with a smile and a handshake, and Sam could see immediately why people called him charismatic. He was more handsome in person than in print ads. Sam was sure the man would look good in front of a television lens with his thick head of light brown hair and sparkling blue eyes that reminded Sam of sapphires.

"Don't know that I ever met a private detective before. Must be a fascinating job," he said.

Sam didn't comment on that, but decided to toss back some charm. "I've heard many wonderful things about your service here," he said as he settled into an office chair.

"Thank you, Mr. Osborne. That's very kind of you. Coffee?"

"No, thank you," Sam replied. "I drank two cups before I left home. That's my limit most days."

He glanced around the office, his eyes settling on a framed picture of a woman. Knowing he was being rude, Sam reached over and picked up the frame.

"Is this your wife?"

A cloud passed quickly across the minister's face. If Sam hadn't been looking for it, he probably wouldn't have noticed.

"Yes, that's Anne. Taken just before she fell ill."

"Oh," Sam said, putting the picture back in the same spot. "I'm sorry. I guess that explains why several people we spoke to commented they'd never met her."

The cloud settled into a slight scowl. The reverend rearranged his body in his chair, joined his hands and laid them on the desk before him.

"We?" the reverend asked. "I thought you were a private detective. Did you come here to question me about my mentally ill wife?"

"Oh no, not at all. I didn't know she was sick." It was a lie. Danny had already told him Anne had been in and out of a local mental health treatment facility several times over the last five years. The reverend didn't need to know how much Sam already knew, just as he didn't need to know that Sam was working with several police forces as well as Carla's mother.

"Actually, I'm here about someone who has attended your church."

The scowl disappeared as quickly as it had come, and the wide-toothed smile of earlier snapped back into place. The reverend formed a steeple with the forefingers of his joined hands and tapped the steeple on his chin.

"Of course. Of course. What can I help you with?"

"Her name is Carla Dunlap. She's a grad student at the University of Richmond, and I'm afraid she's gone missing."

"Yes, I'd heard. What terrible news," the reverend said. The chin tapping stopped and his joined hands came down to rest on the desk, but Sam noted no other change in his demeanor. "Someone sent me a news article from Richmond about it earlier this week. I'm not sure what I can help with, but of course, I know Carla. She's volunteered for several events here at our church."

"Your name came up in the investigation," Sam said, then waited a moment for a reaction. The pleasant expression remained intact; the hands remained entwined on the desk.

"We've been told you were lovers."

Sam got the reaction he sought. Reverend Joe Williams stood abruptly, almost knocking over his chair. The charm was completely gone, and in its place, Sam saw real anger.

"That's a lie. She's just a college student. I'm a married man. I'm a *minister*!"

Sam peered up at the man but did not rise from the office chair.

"Are you saying it isn't true? That you and Carla weren't dating? That you didn't meet up with her in Richmond?"

"I certainly am," the reverend replied. He straightened the front of his shirt and sat back down.

"I suppose you must have talked to someone who spotted us having coffee or dinner here in York. We did that several times," he said. He strummed his fingers on the desk.

"I administer to those in need, Mr. Osborne. Carla had several pressing problems, and she sought out my advice. She traveled all the way from Richmond a few times after church office hours, and I met her at a local restaurant."

"Problems?" Sam repeated.

"I can't tell you about that. It's confidential information."

"So one of them wasn't her heritage or her birth father?"

The remark got no response. Sam could see the reverend now considered himself in charge of the conversation: confidence had returned. Sam did not expect him to lose his cool again—he was too experienced at one-on-one conversations. Joe Williams' television smile was back.

"As I've explained, Mr. Osborne. I cannot talk about what she and I discussed."

"Even if it might help me with this investigation … help me find Carla?"

But Sam could see he was getting no further. The preacher remained silent, saying nothing at all.

Sam studied his notes, then looked up at Joe.

"Do you know an Alice Springer, then, from Winchester. I believe she's been here with Betty Farthing, her friend.

Joe was nodding his head slowly. His forehead wrinkled.

"Yes, I believe I met her not too long ago. But *know* her how? And how is she connected to Carla?"

Sam just studied the man, not about to share anything more, but seeing that he wasn't getting much more either. If the Reverend Joe Williams was having an affair with Carla, if he had any deeper connection with Alice Springer, they'd have to find out on their own. This man wasn't saying anything, and Sam didn't want to give him much more for fear that if he was involved, it might put Carla in danger.

Sam stood and reached across the desk towards Joe's hand.

"It's something unrelated. Listen, I thank you for your time. My apologies for any upset I caused."

Joe stood before grasping Sam's hand and pumping it a few times.

"We all have our duties," he said. "Mine is to administer comfort and teach God's way. Yours is to solve crimes and ask questions. There is nothing to forgive."

Sam shivered as he left the church for his car. The wind had added a chill to the already frosty morning. Snow was starting to fall heavily. However, Sam was pretty sure the sudden cold he felt came as much from meeting the "good" Reverend Williams as the current weather. There was something about the man that felt wrong to Sam.

In the car, he called ahead to Mark in Richmond. The two had agreed to head for Charlottesville that afternoon to talk to the family of the elderly woman who had disappeared.

CHAPTER EIGHTEEN

THE CHILL IN THE AIR turned into frost, freezing some of the roads and causing traffic to back up on 95 South. The trip took almost two hours longer than it should have, and Sam didn't arrive in Richmond until about four-thirty.

Mark waited patiently, having spent the day on the phone and his computer, bringing FBI agent Juarez up to speed, then coordinating efforts and information exchange with the special task force, which now included representatives from other municipalities.

Although it was late in the afternoon, the road icing had cleared, and the detectives agreed to stick with the original plan. After a quick stop at a drive-through for burgers, the two detectives were on their way to Charlottesville. Mark filled Sam in on some of what the Charlottesville police chief had told him.

"Police have checked out the background of the caregiver for Helen Tompkins. She's worked for the family five years—came to them about the time

Helen became confined to a wheelchair. Nothing came up on her background, and her husband and family have vouched for where she was that afternoon—she was home by her usual five-fifteen."

Mark's eyes studied the road ahead.

"As far as the funeral director, however, we've come up against a blank wall. Helen noted only a 'Mr. Smith' and 'Fairhaven,' which was probably the name he gave her for the funeral home, on her calendar at home. Helen owns a cell phone, but left it at home, which her daughter Millie said was a frequent occurrence. Charlottesville police are checking phone records to see if we can pinpoint any calls to a funeral home."

His eyes left the road long enough to connect with Sam's for a moment.

"How in the world did this man convince her to just get in a vehicle with him without letting someone know where she was going to be?"

Sam shrugged.

"I guess she's of the generation that does not consider a smart phone the thread that ties her world together and does not feel she has to be connected twenty-four seven. He invited her for a nice trip out of the house, and she went."

Millie Tompkins met them at the door. She was a thin woman in her early thirties with light brown hair streaked with gold. Her red rimmed eyes showed no surprise at visitors.

"Are you the detectives from Richmond? The police said you'd be by."

Although she reached her hand out towards Mark, then Sam, her idea of a handshake was a quick squeeze. She led the men down a short hallway to the living room, then sank down in an armchair as if she was carrying the burden of her mother's disappearance on her shoulders.

She's had three days of constant worry, Sam thought. *She's got to be exhausted.*

"I know you've reported all this to the police, but can you run over the details for us of who your mom supposedly met with on the day she disappeared?" he said.

Millie ran a palm down the chair's arm, then picked at one spot along that arm. She didn't look at them as she repeated what she'd probably said several times.

"She told me Saturday she'd met this nice man the day before who told her all about a funeral insurance plan sponsored by a new mortuary on the edge of town. She didn't want to be a burden on me or my brother so she decided to see if she could make funeral plans before she passed."

Her gaze finally connected with Sam, and he saw a glimmer of guilt.

"The man volunteered to come and get her and take her to the office. She doesn't get out often enough. What with my husband, the kids and their school schedules …"

Her voice dropped off, as did her gaze. Sam was sure she'd been beating herself up over the fact she'd let her mom go off with a stranger.

"This isn't your fault, Ms. Perkins. Your mom was living independently. She's obviously got her faculties and is capable of making her own decisions," he said.

"Then why does it feel like it is? There's no Fairhaven Funeral Home in Charlottesville. Why didn't I check?"

Millie seemed to sink even lower in her chair.

"This man seemed to know exactly how Mom felt. At least that's what she said when she talked to me Saturday. She said he was very kind and understanding and knew just what she was feeling about being a burden. He was taking her to see the new facility and to pick out a casket and talk about all the arrangements. She actually sounded excited about the outing and I thought: what harm could it do?"

Sam referred to his notes.

"She went out around two and was supposed to be back by four-thirty?"

"That's right. I came by about three to drop off a casserole and her caregiver Becky reminded me she was out at her appointment. I went back home and Becky called about five to say she was leaving on schedule and that Mom wasn't home. When Mom still wasn't answering her landline by dinnertime, I started to worry. She's not good with the cell I bought her, but she's usually good about answering her home phone. I went back to her house and finally called the police about seven-thirty. They sent a patrol car out to talk to me."

Millie's voice cracked and she struggled to sit up in the chair, but dropped her head into her hands instead as if her thoughts had become too heavy.

"Who would take my mom? We have no money; she's old; she's wheelchair bound. She's on all sorts of medicine—including something for her diabetes. What kind of sick person steals a grandma? What will happen to her if she doesn't get her meds?"

Mark flipped through his own notebook to locate a few notes he'd taken earlier.

"The doctors say she'll probably be fine for a while—a little confused maybe. But we don't want you to lose hope. We'll find her if we can," he said.

His words seemed to bring her a small amount of comfort, and she lifted her head to face her visitors.

"Ms. Perkins …. Millie. How did your mother find out about this funeral director?" Sam asked.

"As I told the police, she had a notice she got from somewhere. I supposed I should have checked it out, but I have to allow my mom some freedom. Why would I suspect anything about a funeral director?"

Millie got up and went to a desk and pulled out a piece of paper.

"The police called this number of course. It's no longer in service."

Sam studied the paper and ran a finger over what appeared to be pinholes at the top.

"Do you think she got this notice from a bulletin board?" he asked.

Millie looked confused. "I don't know. I assumed it was a house-to-house flier from the neighborhood."

Mark saw where Sam was going with his questioning.

"Does your mom have a coffee shop or a public place she frequents where she may have picked this up?"

"Yes. Joe's Coffee and Crumble. She and her friends meet there several times a week for coffee. One of her friends usually picks her up."

Sam met Mark's eyes.

"And have you heard of or are you connected in any way to the Reverend Joe Williams of York United Methodist Church?" Sam asked.

Millie paused for a moment, mulling that over.

"I think that's the name of the minister she listens to on Sundays. She doesn't get out to church much. But she sure loves his radio sermons," she said.

As they were walking to a nearby neighbor's house, Sam turned to Mark.

"Didn't Melissa tell you that she thought that the place where someone may have overheard their conversation about Carla's birth father was at the student's hang-out coffee shop?" he asked.

Mark nodded his head.

"And didn't Alice Springer's car give out the first time at a coffee shop?"

"Yep," Mark said.

"Guess our perp, if there's just one, likes his coffee. Or at least he likes what he can find out at a place where others enjoy their brew and conversation," Sam said.

"Yeah, and we now have three connections to the good reverend," Mark added.

The detectives stood on the stoop of the home catty-corner from the Tompkins house. It belonged to Aldo Messinger, the person identified by a police force neighborhood canvas as the only potential witness.

Like Mrs. Tompkins, the man was elderly, but he seemed to get around well. He greeted them at the door himself and invited them in for a chat.

"Like I told the police, it was a lighter-colored van—maybe beige or tan. Kinda dirty really, and it had no writing on the side. Parked a couple houses down on my side of the street. I saw Mrs. Tompkins wheeling across the street talking away to the man as they went, perfectly relaxed."

"How did you happen to see all this?" Mark asked.

"This is a friendly neighborhood. We watch out for each other. I glanced out the window and saw Mrs. Tompkins and this guy and thought it was unusual. She doesn't get out much and it's usually with her friends or her daughter."

Sam looked down at his notes.

"You described him as average weight and height, probably Caucasian, but you weren't sure. You didn't see his hair color?"

"Naw, he was wearing one of those jackets with the things in back. You know like all the kids wear?"

"You mean a hoodie?" Sam asked

"Yeah, that's the one."

Sam's head came up, and he looked over at Mark, noting the question in the other detective's eyes. They were thinking the same thing.

"A funeral director who wears a hoodie?" he said out loud.

"Yeah," Aldo said. "I mean I didn't find out 'til I talked to police that he was supposedly a funeral director. I know it's a much more relaxed atmosphere these days. But why wasn't he in a suit and tie?"

"Anything else odd about him or the situation?" Mark asked.

"Naw. Except ..." Aldo looked out the window as though putting together a memory at just that moment. He pursed his lips, then turned his attention back to the detectives.

"If he was a professional, I was also wondering why his van didn't have one of those lifts. He just up and picked Helen up off her chair and put her in the passenger side. Then put the chair in the van's side door."

As they were walking back to the car, Mark answered his cell phone. He stopped outside the driver's side and began nodding his head as though the person on the other end could see him agreeing. Sam was sure that whatever Mark was learning had something to do with the case. He waited at the passenger side door as the conversation continued.

Mark pressed end and turned to Sam.

"That was Thurgood from my office. He's been doing some digging trying to find this Don Thomas person in Arizona—the other guy Katherine Dunlap identified as a possible father for Carla. It's taken awhile, but they've located an address for someone in Phoenix they believe is Katherine Dunlap's high school acquaintance. He's the right age and Katherine said she thought he'd gone into sales—something to do with jewelry. The Facebook account where she connected with him is old and out-dated, but he's listed in LinkedIn and from the picture, we believe it's the same guy. He works for a small jewelry chain—Smith and Wythe."

Sam opened his door and got in. Mark did the same. Then Sam turned to his new "partner."

"Well, I guess that's good they've located him, but if he's a sales rep in Arizona, that kind of leaves him out of this picture entirely, doesn't it."

Mark grinned.

"Nope. Not really. Smith and Wythe has two offices: one is located in Phoenix; the other is here on the east coast, in downtown Richmond, Virginia. It could just be a coincidence …"

"But we don't believe in coincidences," Sam finished.

CHAPTER NINETEEN

THE STAIN ON THE CEILING had taken on significance—it looked like a woman on her knees praying. The endless stream of religious books must be getting to her. It was the only thing on hand to read, except for the Bible of course. He loved to read passages from the Bible to all of them in the common room.

At least they were all getting a break. He'd been gone nearly two days—no crying through the wall, no scary games of checkers after dinner—games she let him win, not wanting to upset him.

She was truly worried, though, about both the woman in the next room and Maw Maw. She'd heard nothing in the time he was gone. Were they still alive? Were there others besides those two women?

Carla couldn't understand why he treated her like she was a misbehaving daughter and the lady in the other room like a queen—when he wasn't assaulting the poor woman that is. And where was he now? He'd said only one thing before leaving.

"Your Mom needs more than Maw Maw and you. I have to finish this."

Carla was afraid to think about what that meant. Finish as in finish *them*?

Then he'd left, and she was stuck in this room, a box of cereal and several bags of chips her only nourishment. Her wrists were raw from trying to loosen the ropes. The chamber pot was stinking up the corner of the room. A large plastic bottle of water sat at her bedside.

What would happen if he never returned? How long did they say a person could survive without water: three days? Maybe she'd better ration what she had. It was nearly gone.

Was this how her pursuit of love and answers was to end: in starvation or death by thirst?

She had to stop thinking like this. None of it made any sense.

"Hello? Can you hear me out there?" Carla called out. She knew it was no use. She'd even screamed for a while last night when he'd not returned. No one answered.

CHAPTER TWENTY

Friday, November 18

MARK SAT AT HIS DESK, frustrated, and confused. Sam had returned to Lancaster last night and while the two had talked and compared notes, he felt like no one had gotten far enough in the last forty-eight hours with this case. Carla Dunlap had been gone almost two weeks, Alice Springer a week and a half and Helen Tompkins five days. *Were any of them still alive?* Although the FBI had entered the picture and Juarez was using his vast resources, a strong link between the cases hadn't been found. It had to be out there, but he was running out of ideas.

A picture of Melissa Burns crept into his thoughts—the sadness engrained deeply in her blue eyes; how quickly the sadness turned to flame at the mention of someone taking her good friend. Two weeks was a long time for someone to be missing. Would he have to break the bad news to her someday that her roommate wasn't coming back?

Suddenly the image in his head became reality as Melissa walked into his office and plopped down on one of two office chairs, her red curls bouncing, her eyes aflame again. *How had she managed to get by Kathy, the receptionist?*

"I can't keep on pretending nothing has happened," Melissa said without preamble. Her hands went to her hips and she began to rock back and forth. "I can't wait by the phone for news, trying to go to classes I can't concentrate on ... I just can't do this anymore. You have to tell me what's going on."

He calmed his own shock of seeing her materialize with a deep breath, then asked: "How did you manage to get in? They usually buzz us from reception."

Melissa waved away the question.

"I just walked in behind an officer."

Mark blinked. "You just *walked* in. Behind an officer?

Melissa shrugged.

"Surprising what looking like you belong can do. I put my hands behind my back and acted like I was being brought in for something."

She leaned forward, her eyes narrowed as she added, "So, tell me what you've found out. Please."

Mark was amazed. If this young woman hadn't been getting a degree in psychology, he might have suggested acting. She certainly had an expressive face. And apparently, the capability to convince people she was something other than what she was. He should mistrust her. But he didn't.

Mark knew he also should give her the standard lines at this point. *We're doing everything we can. We can't really share the details. We've brought the FBI into the case.* He just couldn't do it. The wheels in her brain needed something to grind on besides the possibility Carla was dead. He got up from his chair and closed the door.

"We're investigating a link between Carla's disappearance and several others in the area," he said, glad his boss couldn't hear him. He trusted his own instincts about Melissa—that she wouldn't talk to the media; that she'd keep the information confidential if he asked. But his ass could be on the line for even sharing that much.

He returned to his chair and looked up to see huge, terror-filled eyes. With a shaky voice, she said, "you think it's a serial killer."

Dang, he was digging himself in deep here. He shook his head.

"Don't jump to that conclusion, Miss Burns. It may be a good thing that the disappearances occurred so close together. If they are indeed linked, there may be something else going on. We have to consider the possibility that there is a purpose to what this perp or perps are doing."

That seemed to calm her just a bit. She sat thinking for a moment.

"You still think it's linked to the news about her father?"

"We're checking several angles there as well, but my best guess is that yes, it's an important part of what's happened," Mark said.

"And what about Carla's minister boyfriend. I keep going back to him and their affair. It was just so unlike Carla to date a married man. Do you think he's involved in all this?"

"We've talked to him. The FBI has talked to him. He has an alibi for where he was when Carla was taken. And he claims consistently there was no affair and that Carla and he were just friends, or rather, confessor and confessee. We can't find proof they were having an affair, though I did get June Grindage to admit Carla mentioned having feelings for him," Mark said. "And of course, there's what Carla told you as well."

He wasn't ready to share with her the fact that Alice Springer and Helen Tompkins also had connections with the reverend.

Melissa rose from her seat. "He has to know something. I just know he does. I'm going to go talk to him myself. I have to know." She grabbed her purse from the desk, turned toward his office door.

Before she could reach for the knob, Mark said simply: "*Stop.*" She turned back to him, breathing heavily, a question in her eyes.

"Just sit down please," he said calmly.

She returned to her chair, her chin jutted out, her arms crossed.

What could he say to get her to think more rationally? He would never forgive himself if something happened to this little firecracker of a woman.

"You can't go in there, guns ablaze and accusations on your tongue. You need to leave this to the police. Did I make a mistake sharing information with you?"

She said nothing, but he saw her jaw relax; her arms uncross and come down to her sides.

"If he's indeed involved in some way, he could be dangerous. He already knows he's a person of interest in this case," Mark said. "If you alert him to the fact you knew about an affair, it might anger him. I'm not sure what he would do."

That seemed to make her think. She rubbed her forehead with one hand, then sat back as an idea seemed to gel.

"What if he doesn't know why I'm there?"

Mark's brows drew together. "What do you mean?"

"He's never met me, Detective Brady. What's to keep me from attending his church, maybe staying for the social afterwards and 'getting to know' the good preacher?"

She tugged at her lower lip, giving herself a moment to rationalize.

"I might be able to find out some little tidbit. At least it would give me something to do; some way to help, however small. There's nothing illegal about going to church, right?"

Mark played with the stapler on his desk. He couldn't blame her for wanting to help. If it had been his good friend missing, he knew he couldn't sit back and wait for action. His eyes rose from the stapler to Melissa's face.

God, she has the cutest freckles. Why am I thinking about her freckles?

He picked up the stapler and put it back down with just enough force to get her attention.

"Look. I can't keep you from attending the church. But he doesn't know me either," the words were tumbling out faster than his rational mind could process.

"How about I pick you up at six Sunday morning, and we'll go together armed with a story—we can pretend to be a couple; someone who knew Carla. I'm not sure how we'll work that into a social conversation, but we can plan on the way. It's supposed to be a good day for a drive. Clear and much warmer."

She tilted her head and gave him a lopsided grin. "Are you asking me out on a date?"

Mark could feel his cheeks turning red. *What the hell did I just do?* But Melissa laughed.

"Relax, Detective. I'm just teasing. I would very much appreciate having you along. But I *do* insist on buying you lunch or brunch afterwards. We may as well make a day of it."

It was a wonderful sound, the tinkle of her laugh. He'd given her a moment's respite from worry. Even if it wasn't entirely proper for him to go along, didn't she deserve that?

"I have a better idea," Mark said. "Why don't you join me for Sunday dinner that night. My sister Janet has me over to her house most Sundays. I'm sure she'd love the added company."

Melissa rose, picked up her purse again.

"That sounds lovely, Detective Brady. I'll see you then."

"The name is Mark. Mark Brady. If we're going to be a couple for a day, we should be on a first name basis."

He watched her go, a small smile on his face. Her 'plan' was amateur and probably wouldn't net much. But it gave him an excuse to be in a car with her for most of a day.

Sunday, November 20

Sunday turned out as predicted: an uncharacteristically warm December day that directly contrasted with the ice and snow of just a few days before. Mark and Melissa headed to York in Mark's old BMW, coffee, and scones from a local Starbucks in hand.

Mark saw the drive as an opportunity to get to know her better. Even if he shouldn't be going out with anyone involved in a case, especially someone so close to the victim, this was different, wasn't it? It wasn't really a date—he was fact gathering. But he smiled to himself. Why lie? He was also very attracted to this woman.

"It might help us act more like a couple to get to know a little about each other, don't you think?" he said.

"M-m-m," she said. "I was thinking it would be fun to be someone brand new. An exotic dancer returned to the folds of the church. You could be the man who saved me from my sins by dragging me to church." He whipped his head around. *Was she serious?*

She chuckled and put her fingertips to her mouth, sobering.

"O-*kay*. I suppose your approach is a better one," she said, letting her hand drop into her lap. "A couple it is." She focused her attention on his face. "So, where were you born?"

"I've always thought it was Munson Hospital near Traverse City, Michigan," Mark said without thinking.

"Always thought?" Melissa echoed.

Ah, the psychologist in her had picked up on something. Mark didn't feel like explaining the slip though. He wasn't sure why he'd put it that way anyway. He was just missing a birth certificate and some pictures. As soon as his schedule allowed, he'd track them down. Feeling suddenly vulnerable, he adopted the formal tone he used in briefings.

"My two siblings and I were born in Michigan where my family used to live. I grew up in the Traverse City, Michigan area. My dad died about six years ago. Mom passed away just a few months ago.

"From Traverse, I moved to Washington, D.C. to study law enforcement after getting an associates' degree back home. I got my master's last year. This is my third on-the-force job and the first as an official detective. I have one sister who moved to this area before me and a brother back home."

He felt her eyes on his face. "I'm sorry about your mom," she said. "What a tough year for you and your siblings."

Then she was quiet, as though thinking about what she'd just said.

In a soft voice she added, "What's it like to have two siblings?"

Mark took his eyes off the road again to glance her way. She sat, her head bent, hands knitted and resting in her lap. He knew from the report he'd pulled her parents were a local couple who had adopted her. They had no other children. Was it loneliness he heard in her voice?

"You wanted a larger family?"

"I may have siblings out there," she said, lifting her head to gaze out her window. "I'll never know. I was in the foster care program when I was a baby, and my records are sealed."

Her eyes returned to his face.

"Don't get me wrong, though. I was one of the lucky ones. I ended up with great foster parents who adopted me when I was about five. They're wonderful and I have nothing to complain about. I love them very much. They just didn't have any kids themselves, and I always thought it would be great to be part of a larger family."

"Oh. Okay," Mark said. "I never thought of my family as big, but compared to one child, I guess it feels that way."

He tried a reassuring smile.

"I did grow up close to my siblings," he said. "I'm the oldest. My brother Bill is a couple of years younger. He and I are nothing alike—not in personality or looks or even in lifestyle. We've always gotten along really well though. He's kind of an urban, artsy type—lives near downtown Traverse. He's a freelance writer by trade."

"And your sister?" she said.

Mark let the question linger, thinking about Janet, his best friend. His thoughts brought another smile to his lips.

"Janet was the baby of the family; the adored child who could do no wrong. But then again, she didn't *do* much of *any*thing wrong. Never in trouble. Always responsible. These days, she acts more like my mom, which I'm sure you'll discover this afternoon when we visit her."

Mark decided to trip the reverse switch.

"So, how did you end up in Richmond?" he asked.

She paused for several moments, gazing at him as if measuring why he didn't particularly like talking about himself. But her eyes went back to the dashboard in front of her as she began to talk.

"I came for the school's psychology undergrad program, stayed for grad school and really kind of like it in the city. My parents still live in Gordonsville, Virginia—population a whopping 1,600. It's a little too small for my taste."

Her words sounded rehearsed as though she'd been asked that question many times, which he supposed she had: probably from every date she'd had in the last few years.

She offered no more data, however, and he was just wondering why she'd grown quiet when she said:

"Hey, what should we say that you do for a living when we're asked?"

Mark laughed, breaking through the quiet tension.

"I guess it wouldn't do to be a detective investigating a murder the preacher has been questioned about, huh?" Mark said. "I probably shouldn't get too far from the truth though—I'm not that great of a liar."

Melissa reached out to pat his shoulder, and he looked over to see her grinning.

"Don't say that as if it's a fault, Detective. I know *way* too many guys who are very good at it."

He chuckled and saluted her, showing he understood.

"Let's say I'm in security then. It's partly true. I have an occasional weekend gig filling in for a buddy at a local apartment complex, and I worked security while I was pursuing my studies."

He tripped his blinker and changed lanes, then glanced over her way again.

"And what do I say about you, *girlfriend*. Or are we married?"

They both laughed that time.

"I supposed I should stick close to the truth, too, though I'm not too bad a liar."

"Ah, something most people don't boast about," Mark said.

"It can come in handy, that's for sure, but I try not to practice the skill too often," she said. She gazed back out her side of the car, and he suddenly pictured her admitting the truth about Carla and her affair. Were there other things she hadn't told him?

She didn't give him much time to let the thought settle, however, before continuing her planning.

"How about I say I'm a student—a stay-at-home wife pursuing education at night. Trying to start our family."

The words seemed to bring back the tension, however. The lighthearted tone was completely gone when she added:

"Or we could just be engaged and forget the kids." Melissa was staring out her side of the car.

"Do you want a big family then?" *Now why did I toss out that question. It's really none of my business,* Mark thought. But he did wonder why her mood had darkened.

Melissa turned back to him. She didn't appear upset with the question, but maybe a bit surprised he would ask it. Her chin came up.

"Well, me as the fake Melissa, your fiancée, only wants one boy and one girl. The real Melissa, however, wants a gazillion kids and I do not care what sex they are."

Mark laughed from deep within his gut. *She really is a refreshing drink of water.*

The two arrived in time for the second service of the morning at ten-thirty. They sat in the back, but made sure to shake the preacher's hand on the way out the door and mention that they were new parishioners. As expected, Reverend Williams invited the new couple to the after-service social.

Half an hour later, they were sipping coffee in the church basement when the minister walked up to them to welcome them into his congregation.

Mark studied him as he approached them and thought: it's probably hard for most people to image the minister as someone who might have a secret girlfriend he may have harmed. Joe Williams was tall and solidly built, and Mark could imagine many women found the perfectly coiffed light brown hair, the dark blue eyes, and the very white teeth handsome. Reverend Williams seemed genuinely warm in his greeting and his questioning; like he really wanted to get to know the couple. Mark also realized, however, that really good criminals were some of the most seemingly sincere con artists out there.

"So you work in security huh? Somewhere around here I presume?" the reverend said to Mark.

Mark and Melissa had already worked this part of their background story out and shared it with Reverend Williams at the after-service hand-shaking line. Since Mark now knew just enough of Lancaster from the visit with Sam, he'd given the town as their residence and his place of employment.

Before getting an answer to "around here I presume?", however, the reverend turned to Melissa. "And you're a grad student at Millersville? That must keep you both busy. I hope you'll have time to help us in one of the many volunteer opportunities here at the church."

"I'm almost done with my studies—then maybe," Melissa said. "I just have an internship to do in Richmond." She set her coffee down and grabbed Mark's arm for a squeeze.

"Three months away from him. I don't know how I'll stand it," she said, beaming at her "fiancé." The touch of her fingers and the enthusiasm in her face gave Mark a jolt that almost felt like hunger. Did he wish it was true?

She turned back to the preacher, and Mark sensed her refocus her enthusiasm on the reverend's face.

"Ever been there?"

"To Richmond?" the preacher asked. His handsome features showed no hint of surprise at the question, and Mark wondered if he practiced calmness in the mirror. He guessed it might come in handy with such a public role.

"Yeah," Melissa said. "Just wondering what kind of city I face. Whether there's traffic to contend with. I've lived around here most of my life."

His tone did not change as he said: "I don't think I've been to Richmond often enough to render an opinion. But I do have a parishioner or two that hails from that area."

"They drive all the way for Sunday service?" Mark said. He knew he sounded a bit skeptical, but it was a fair question—they'd just made that drive in four-and-a-half hours.

The reverend turned back to Mark, the glow of his smile not even flickering.

"I don't see them every week of course. I'm not sure what a couple of them do on a regular basis, but I have one person who goes to our sister church in Richmond most Sundays."

Bingo. Mark thought. Carla attended Discovery United Methodist near the university. The reverend was likely referring to her.

Melissa rested her chin on one palm and leaned a little closer towards him, drawing his attention back her way. The gesture made her seem like an adoring teenager talking to her idol. She really was a good actress.

"Since I'm going to be there for a few months, maybe I can go to that church, too," Melissa said, a bit breathless. "I'll be staying in west Richmond. The internship is connected to the University of Richmond."

Mark could see from the slight shift in the minister's posture that the reference to the college had poked a nerve. He said nothing about Carla or the fact he knew her and that she'd gone missing, but he looked over her shoulder as if seeking someone else to talk to.

"Say, maybe you can let her know I'll be interning in her area, and she can show me around," Melissa said.

Reverend Williams' face remained impassive, but he raised his brows and looked back at both of them. He'd caught the gender reference.

"She?"

Melissa giggled, maintaining the teenage image. She covered her mouth with a hand as if embarrassed by her blunder.

"Oh. I'm sorry," she said, dropping the hand, "I guess I shouldn't have assumed. It's a guy then? Well, maybe he can at least introduce me to the church."

Mark watched the reverend put down his coffee cup on a nearby table, a gesture he was pretty sure meant the man was moving on to another couple and perhaps a more comfortable conversation.

To delay that, Mark glanced around the basement hall and asked: "Is your wife here? Can we meet her?"

He saw Reverend Williams shoulders stiffen, his eyes narrow slightly, his nostrils flare. Yet Mark knew it was another fair question: Carla and Mark were supposedly new parishioners and most preachers had wives that were an integral part of the church's ministries.

"My wife has been ill," Joe Williams said.

"Oh, I'm so sorry," Melissa said, reaching out to touch his forearm. "Has she got that bug that's been going around then? I had it a couple weeks ago, and I can tell you, it leaves you feeling like you'd love nothing better than to just lay in bed with the covers over your head."

"I'm afraid it's a little more complicated than that," Reverend Williams said. He stretched his chin up to glance over her shoulder again. "Excuse me, I need to say hello to the Pattersons."

The reverend had let himself off the hook, and Mark couldn't blame him. He would know that if the engaged couple became involved with the church, they'd soon learn on their own about his wife's condition. The reverend saw no need to bring it up himself.

Mark and Melissa found two other opportunities during the hour-long social to say a few words to Reverend Williams, but they found out little else. He was a polished schmoozer, throwing out three questions to every one they managed to toss his way.

They used the rest of their time to get to know some of the other church attendees, who had nothing but positive words about the man.

"Reverend Joe has changed my life forever. My business has completely turned around since I gave myself over to God," Alan Monopolis said. He was a local businessman with a bad toupee and a religious zeal who had convinced himself 'Reverend Joe' had a direct line to Heaven and that God was on the other end of phone, anxious to hear about the success of Monopolis Enterprises. Mark and Melissa moved as quickly as they could to another conversation.

They gently prodded about the wife.

"Yes, it's a shame about the wife really. I've only met her a few times, and she seemed nice enough. Very quiet and kind of mousy. But a proper lady. I heard, however, that she tipped the bottle a little too much. The poor Reverend." This came from Mrs. Ivory Barest, a blue-haired elderly woman Mark was sure never missed a service or a bit of gossip. Like many of the women Mark and Melissa talked to, she seemed to have a bit of a crush on the reverend.

In contrast to Ivory, Twilla Johnson was a glassy-eyed, smooth-skinned twenty-something. Her face lit up the same way, however, when talking about Reverend Joe Williams.

"He says so many wonderful things. I feel like I bring all of my woes to church with me each Sunday and lay them at his feet." She sighed deeply and bowed her head like she was praying. Melissa caught Mark's attention over the woman's head, then rolled her eyes. He put a hand to his mouth to hide a smile.

Iris Clark, a middle-aged woman whose faded beauty wasn't really brightened by the healthy dose of makeup or the heavy floral scent, was another of his admirers. "He does so much good in our community. He comes with me to see my mom in the nursing home at least once a month. I don't know what I'd do without his support."

On the way out the door, Melissa took a last opportunity for a word with the reverend. She handed him a piece of paper with the 'junk' email address she used only for shopping online.

"Maybe you can let me know your Richmond parishioner's number and once I'm settled, I'll see if we can attend church together," she said.

Reverend Williams tucked the paper away in a pocket. "I'll have to check with her first, of course. I believe she said she was going out of town," he said.

Neither Mark nor Melissa said much for the first ten minutes of the drive back to Richmond. Mark guessed they were both absorbing and analyzing what they'd learned. It hadn't been much, but it had kept her from plowing into dangerous territory on her own.

He glanced over to see Melissa staring out the front, her body stiff, her hands folded in her lap. After the animated cheerfulness she'd assumed for their ruse, it seemed wrong to see her so rigid.

"What?" he asked. "What are you thinking?"

She slowly turned her head his way, capturing him with her eyes. The fear was back and it hit Mark in the chest. He wanted so badly to rid the world of that look.

"Do you think she told him something she couldn't tell me? That she really just up and left?"

Mark shook his head.

"You *know* Carla, Melissa. You've known her five years. What do you think?"

She toyed with the cross pendant at her neck, sliding it back and forth on its chain as she weighed and discarded possible scenarios.

"Maybe she was pregnant and went off to have the baby. Maybe they're planning some kind of life together in a distant paradise." Mark could sense in her tone, however, that she didn't really believe it.

"But you're right, I know her. And I believe that if either of those were true, there's no way she'd take off without letting me and her mother know she was safe."

She bowed her head and closed her eyes, either praying or just thinking things through.

"And what does your psychology-trained brain tell you about the good Reverend Joe?" Mark asked.

Her eyes opened and she turned his way.

"I think he's an egocentric personality with narcissistic tendencies. Someone who's listened to the praise and adoration of his parishioners and built his world around that."

Her fingers went back to playing with the pendant.

"I do think it's interesting that he admitted his parishioner was a *she* after questioning me on it. And did you notice his hesitancy when I mentioned the university? But I don't know why he said that about her leaving town."

"Me either," Mark said. "He's been questioned about Carla's disappearance. I guess it was just to keep from having to explain who he was talking about."

The worry that flickered across her features triggered a response. He reached over and laid a comforting hand on her forearm.

"We don't even have confirmation the two were involved. There are certainly enough women in that church who seemed to adore the man. Maybe Carla made more of their relationship than actually existed."

But he could see she didn't believe it. Her eyes returned to the road.

"And maybe he's just a weak man whose mentally ill wife gave him an excuse to seek the affections of another woman," she said.

Maybe more than one woman, Mark thought, promising himself he'd look into it.

CHAPTER TWENTY-ONE

JANET FLUNG open her front door and enveloped her brother in a bear hug. She was a few inches taller than Mark, and had a willowy figure, light brown hair and fine features compared to Mark's compact, muscled physique and darker coloring.

Over Mark's shoulder, Janet spotted Melissa standing awkwardly on the bottom step.

"Hello. You must be Melissa." She stepped around Mark and reached for Melissa's hand, then drew the two inside and began a tour of her home. Janet had an eclectic mix of old and new: antiques adorned many of the rooms, but the big pieces of furniture were sturdy and comfortable, more modern. Everywhere you looked were touches of the unusual: an old pinball machine in the basement rec room; a fishing pole fastened to a wall that had picture frames hanging under it. One of the pictures featured three grinning kids holding up fish.

Melissa turned to Mark and poked him in the side.

"You three?" she asked, He laughed and nod-ded.

Nothing seemed expensive in the home, but nothing was cheap either. Somehow everything seemed to go together, at least for Mark. He loved his sister's house.

Echoing Mark's thoughts, Melissa said, "You have a great place here. I really like your taste."

They'd reach the end of the tour and were standing now in the great room. It was a high-vaulted large space with family room seating at one end and the kitchen at the other. Like the rest of the house, the kitchen had touches of old and new: sleek stainless-steel appliances married with an old farmhouse table still wearing its battle scars of scratches.

The seating area contained a leather sofa and overstuffed armchairs. A large man with a head of brown curls looked up from the book he was reading on the couch, the green of his eyes magnified by his glasses.

"And this is another fixture in the house … my husband Ben," Janet said.

Ben got up and stretched, laid his book down and offered Mark a beer.

"And what can I get you, Melissa? I have a bottle of wine chilling or some soda?"

"A beer would be great," Melissa said.

"My kind of gal," Ben said as he left to get the beer.

The four settled in the great room with their refreshments.

"So," Janet said, studying them over the top of a glass of iced tea. "Mark tells me you're from around here? That he's helping you with a case?"

"My parents live in Gordonsville. I'm a grad student at U of Richmond—been here a couple of years." She didn't refer to Carla, and Mark suspected she didn't really want to talk about it; she'd said in the car that today's long, but pleasant drive was first time she'd been able to relax and get away from the stress, at least for part of the ride.

"What are you studying?" Ben asked.

"Psychology. I should have my master's degree later this year, then I've applied for an internship with the Richmond Women's Center. I'm hoping to turn that internship into a job."

Mark raised his brows. "You've got it all planned out then," he said. They hadn't talked much about her future plans—they'd spent too much of the drive getting caught up on the past and creating a false story.

"I'm not very organized about the little things in life," she said. Mark pictured Carla's and Melissa's messy apartment. "But I'm pretty good about the big things. My mom says I've been planning my adulthood since a few years after they adopted me," she said.

"Oh, you're adopted?" Janet said. "Since you were a baby?"

"My parents fostered me from the age of three to about five, then legally adopted me," Melissa said. "I don't know who my birth parents are."

Janet got up to stir something in the kitchen. Ben must have decided they'd pried enough. He rose from his seat and excused himself to get another beer, slugging Mark on the shoulder as he left.

"We always thought this one might be adopted, too," he said.

"What did Ben mean by that remark about you being adopted?" Melissa asked Mark three hours later. They'd just arrived back at Melissa's apartment and Mark had walked her to the door. It had been a comfortable afternoon into evening of conversation, a few beers and Janet's spicy sweet chicken chili. Mark was glad they hadn't gone to a restaurant. He'd learned more about her from Janet and Bill's gentle queries: she'd been driven in school and had known what she wanted to do at a fairly young age. She finished her undergrad studies six months early and pursued her master's in just eight months.

He doubted she'd had much time for dating, a thought that didn't displease him.

"I hope he didn't offend you with that remark," Mark said.

"Of course not. I'm certainly not ashamed to have been adopted."

She fished in her purse, then found what she sought: her apartment key. She held it in her palm as she looked up at Mark.

"I'm just curious why he said it," Melissa said.

"Bill and Janet made it their life's mission to tease me about my appearance," Mark explained. "They were both chips off the old block—they looked like Mom and Dad—tall and thin to my short and stocky. Though I didn't get the family physique, I was also the only athlete in the house. Played a lot of high school football, some baseball, some track."

"Yeah, I could see that from Janet's family pictures." She turned to the door, key in hand. Mark wished she'd invite him in. But it was late, it had been a long day and they were just getting to know each other.

Before inserting the key, she turned back to face him.

"It seemed to bother you though," she said. "Am I wrong?"

He could feel her studying his face and suddenly he was uncomfortable with her reading his mind. *Maybe going out with a psychologist isn't such a good thing.* The thought irritated him—made him mad at himself. They were *not* dating, at least not yet.

"I'm used to it," he said. Her gaze didn't waiver, and the pressure of it pushed him into sharing his concerns.

"I can't find my birth certificate," he blurted out. "After Mom died, the three of us went through all the family papers. I was searching for my certificate because I need a passport. The papers are pretty disorganized, but I could find Bill's and Janet's. Mine wasn't there."

"Well, it's a pretty simple process to reapply to get a birth certificate," Melissa pointed out.

"I know. I know. I've just been busy and the trip isn't for a while, so I haven't gotten around to it." He could hear how flimsy the words were when said out loud. And she continued to study his face.

"There's more," she said.

He let his eyes connect with hers and felt a sudden warmth. He wasn't sure why, but they seemed to be on the same level—they saw things the same way. It was as if she'd been there in his mind all his life and he was just now finding his way to her. He knew he couldn't tell her anything but the truth.

"I also can't find any baby pictures, and this all had me thinking about things. I remember looking at pictures of Bill as a baby and there are hundreds of baby pictures of Janet. But nothing of me. Don't you think that's a bit strange?"

"I think it's just as important that *you* think it's strange. You're a detective. If this is bothering you … detect!" she said.

Mark smiled. She was right of course.

CHAPTER TWENTY-TWO

JAMIE WHITE was twelve years old, and he was tired of being mistaken for someone much younger. His mom told him he had a condition when he was a baby that caused him to grow slower, and that maybe he'd catch up to the rest of the kids one day.

He didn't care about one day: Jamie was just sick of being small. He couldn't keep up with the other boys, so he didn't play sports. The girls all seemed to like him, but they patted him on his head as if he were their adorable younger brother.

Jamie spent most of his time alone, which he didn't really mind because he loved to read, almost as much as he loved to take things apart, then put them together again. Besides, he had an entire world of friends he'd made on the computer and with his cell phone. Snapchat and Instagram didn't reveal how small he was—only what he looked like, and he'd been careful not to post pictures of himself with anybody else. He was pretty good at getting goofy shots of just himself, and he was proud of how many likes he got. Jamie now spent a good portion of every day emailing and instant messaging on the computer or texting the friends he'd made online while playing games or chatting. They were mostly people who didn't go to his school.

Jamie loved his mom and dad, but he wished they wouldn't worry so much. They were constantly urging him to join school clubs or get involved in group activities. But while Jamie knew he was smart, and he liked learning things, he didn't like being in school. Even his teachers treated him as if he was just a kid, and sometimes they just didn't see his hand when it went up. He was usually sitting behind someone bigger.

This morning, Jamie popped out of bed early as he often did. He never could understand people who stayed in bed as long as they could. There was too much to see and do to waste it lying on your back.

He spent the first hour and a half killing zombies in a new computer game he'd discovered. He texted his friend Billy who had discovered the same game and told him how awesome it was.

When he got hungry, he made his own breakfast, something his mom had allowed him to do ever since his twelfth birthday. She was one of the ones who liked staying in bed, and she was rarely up when he left for school. He usually watched the sunrise out the kitchen window while he ate his cheerios or toast.

His dad would stop in the kitchen to fill his travel mug and kiss Jamie on his way out the door to his job. Jamie would wait for that kiss, then pack up his backpack with the lunch Mom had made the night before and the books he needed for the day, and head out the door.

Jamie lived seven blocks from the school, though he often went a few more blocks out of his way just to avoid a couple of bullies who sought him out. As he walked, he texted or checked messages, rarely even looking up. He could travel all of his routes to school with his eyes closed if he had to.

When Jamie came to the park, he saw the old man—Mr. Tom—sitting on the same bench he'd rested on the last few weeks, sipping his coffee. The man smiled warmly and waved with his free hand, so Jamie sat down beside him for a chat. Mr. Tom hadn't been around the last few days. Jamie liked the man because he talked to him like an adult, laughing when Jamie joked about his Instagram friends and acting interested when Jamie talked about his games even though Jamie suspected Mr. Tom was too old to play on a computer. They never spoke long—Jamie knew the man was not so old he didn't have a job. The guy just liked having his morning coffee on this bench.

Today, Jamie talked about zombies, but after only a few minutes, a light drizzle began. The drizzle quickly turned into rain, and Jamie rose to leave. He didn't have an umbrella.

"You'll be soaked," Mr. Tom said. "Let me give you a ride to school."

Jamie knew not to get into a car with a stranger, but Mr. Tom wasn't a stranger, was he? Still, Jamie stood for a moment thinking until they both got really wet.

He's an old man: maybe fifty or forty. I don't want him getting sick. He shouldn't be standing here in the rain.

Jamie got in the car. Mr. Tom drove for a couple blocks towards the school, and Jamie relaxed, glad to have the ride.

Before they reached the school, however, Mr. Tom pulled to the curb. "I'm very warm. I need a sip of water," he said. He took a bottle of water out of the glove compartment, then a handkerchief out of his pocket.

He's going to mop the rain from his face, Jamie thought. But Mr. Tom wetted the handkerchief with water from the bottle, then asked if Jamie wanted a drink.

Jamie shook his head 'no' and suddenly things didn't feel right. The water in the bottle smelled funny. Why did Mr. Tom need a wet cloth when he was already wet? The man had a strange glint in his eye. Jamie tried to reach for the door handle, but the handkerchief was suddenly at his nose and covering his mouth and he couldn't breathe. The day turned into blackness.

"Good boy," Mr. Tom said to the sleeping form. The car took off from the curb.

CHAPTER TWENTY-THREE

Monday, November 21

THE RAIN WAS POUNDING the earth, beating down so hard it was difficult to see. Mark got his umbrella out of the back seat and prepared to make his way to Melissa's door; they were going to dinner. He knew he shouldn't—it was too close to a real date this time, even though she'd initiated it. But he'd had another frustrating day of trying to connect the dots, and when she'd called at lunch with the excuse of inviting him to a 'thank-you' dinner, he didn't have the will to say no.

He thirsted for the company of this spirited woman who somehow made him feel he was doing exactly what he should be doing. Talking to her was like talking to Janet—nutrition for the soul. Except it really went beyond that.

It's more like taking a long cool drink after walking through the desert. He grinned at the thought. How stupid was he being about her?

He was just about to get out of the car, when he spotted his long cool drink, which had quickly become more of a short, drowned rat in the fury of the storm. She came dashing through the rain towards the car, struggling against the wind and losing the battle with an umbrella that had turned inside out.

She hopped in and brought the storm with her—dripping water all over his upholstery.

"Why in the world did you come out here? I would have come to the door," he said.

"I got out of class a little late and haven't been up to the apartment yet. I spotted your car, and it was closer."

The rain had tamed the curls Mark had imagined were unconquerable: her locks lay flat against her head.

She looked down at the car floor and realized she was getting his front seat soaked. "I'm sorry," she said.

"Don't be," he said, and started the car. He turned the heat on high to warm his passenger.

"Wow!" she said. "I don't know that I've ever seen it rain so hard. I'm completely drenched. We may have to forego the trip out until this dies down and I have a chance to go upstairs to change my clothes. I certainly can't go to a restaurant like this."

Mark grinned again. "I have a better idea. I know of a place where you can get dry, change into something comfortable and not have to face any other people. The food isn't great–but the chef tries hard, and he could use the practice."

"Your place," she said. She squeezed a lock of hair, watching as the water dripped onto the floor.

Suddenly he was worried he was being too forward.

"I'm sorry. I just thought with the rain and all, I'd offer up my place. You can take me to that fancy place another time."

She turned to study his face, and he saw the question in her eyes: *another time?* But instead of asking, she laughed.

"Sure. Why not."

The driving was difficult and conversation impossible as the rain continued its vicious attack on the Earth. Mark managed to keep the car on the road, but chastised himself for leaving the apartment and putting them both in this situation. Luckily, there was little traffic probably because of the rain, and as they grew nearer to his home, and the roads became familiar, his grip on the steering wheel relaxed. At last, he turned into a driveway, pushed a button above his head and drove into a garage where the rain finally couldn't get to them.

"Whew," Melissa said.

"Home sweet home," Mark added. His shoulders relaxed, and he faced his guest and saw that the curls had started to dry in the short amount of drive time and were bouncing back to life. He also realized he'd been so intent on the road, he hadn't seen that her clothes were plastered to her body.

Melissa followed his gaze and glanced downward. Her cotton blouse had been turned by water into a peekaboo.

He averted his face and said, "Don't worry, Janet keeps a few things in my spare room."

He was careful not to let his eyes wander over her body as they left the car and headed into the house.

Ten minutes later, Melissa was wearing a warm, dry pair of sweats, and Mark was stirring something on the stove.

"That smells heavenly, but how in the world did you throw it together so quickly?"

"Ah. Good question. I could lie to you and tell you that gourmet cooking is one of my many talents …"

Melissa slugged him on the shoulder.

"You're not that good at lying, remember?"

She cocked one hip at him and laughed. He smiled in return, then took up a spoon and dipped into what he was cooking, blew on it and held it out towards her. She closed her eyes and breathed in the heady aroma of onions, garlic, tomatoes, then opened her eyes and took the spoon from his hand. The tip of her tongue came out to taste the dish, and her lids closed again to absorb the pleasure. They fluttered open and found his face, and he felt a moment of desire at her reaction. He really wanted to kiss her.

"Spaghetti Bolognese," she said, breaking the spell. "How did you do it?"

He turned away to steady himself and began picking up the counter, just to have somewhere to look besides into those deep blue eyes. As he worked he talked, trying keep his tone casual and friendly.

"The secret to this gourmet cook's success is a sister who's willing to trade portions from her culinary expertise for my handiness around a home. Her husband is useless with a tool. She bribes me with food. I have a big freezer. If left on my own, I'd probably live on what McDonald's has on its menu."

Mark poured two glasses of wine and handed her a plate, then sat across from her. He watched her take a generous portion of noodles, ladle out the rich sauce, then pick up her fork and a spoon. Twirling the pasta, she lifted fork to lips without spilling even a drop of the sauce and plopped the whole thing into her mouth.

"Say, you're pretty good at that. Think you might have some Italian blood in you?" he said.

She grinned and shrugged but continued to chew. She was through two more forkfuls when she finally paused, laid down her fork and sighed. Then she grabbed a crusty roll, broke off a piece of bread and slathered it with butter.

"That sister of yours can cook," she said. "I hope you fixed a lot of doorknobs to get this."

He spat out a piece of bread laughing at her remark, then put his napkin to his mouth to hide his embarrassment. Patting a few times, he laid it down, hoping she'd missed his crudeness.

"She told me she'd teach me to cook someday, but someday doesn't ever seem to get here," he said.

She must have thought he was berating himself because she leaned over and touched his arm. "That doesn't mean you'll never have time, Mark. What with trying to save the world and help poor damsels in distress like me, of course it's hard to find minutes for the simpler things in life."

He smiled at her then, and she smiled back, and the light in the room seemed to brighten by a few kilowatts.

When the spaghetti was mostly gone, Mark got up, grabbed their plates, and put them in the sink.

"Let's go to the living room, and I'll build us a fire."

After Mark stacked the wood, lit it, and stepped away from the blaze, they sat side by side on the couch, admiring his handiwork and finishing their wine.

"There is absolutely nothing homier than a fire in the fireplace," Melissa said.

"Agreed," Mark said. "It's a simple thing I *always* find time for."

They both sighed and stared into the fire.

"Melissa?" Mark said after a few minutes.

"M-m-m h-m-m?" she said.

He reached over and put his wine glass on the table.

His action caught her attention, and she turned questioning eyes from the fire to his face.

"I called Munson Hospital today to try to find out what happened to my birth records," he said.

"Oh?"

"I did it because when people lose a birth certificate, they usually can get one from the Department of Vital Statistics. The agency had no record of me and suggested I try the hospital next—that maybe it didn't get filed properly or something happened."

She straightened in her spot on the sofa, now fully alert to the gravity of what he was saying.

"Munson Hospital, where my mom said I was born, also has no record of a Mark Brady coming into the world on March 3, 1992."

Melissa put her wine glass beside his on the table and turned towards him.

"That's really weird, Mark. What do you suppose happened?"

"I haven't really had time to absorb this. I don't know why my mom would tell me we were all born at that hospital if we weren't. The thing is … I know I had a certificate. I got both my social security card and my driver's license using it. Mom got me the social security card, and I didn't pay attention either time to what hospital was on the certificate. I've had at least two background checks to get jobs and nothing got flagged."

He stretched out his hand and picked his glass back up, studying the rim, not taking a sip.

"But, it's like I don't exist."

Melissa reached out and touched the hand that held his wine glass. He put the glass back down and grabbed her hand, not knowing why, just needing the touch. Their entwined hands rested on the couch between them. It felt good to be able to share his doubts with someone, even if he didn't yet know her well.

"Do you think something's going on there? Do you think your parents lied to you?" she asked.

"I can't imagine that. It wasn't their style. I don't know what's going on. I intend to find out."

Both of them were now studying their joined hands. He relaxed his grip, but didn't let go. It didn't feel at all wrong or out of place. However, he felt her shiver.

"Are you cold?"

"No," she said. "Not at all."

Their gazes slowly rose from their hands to each other's face.

"Are you ever going to kiss me?" Melissa whispered.

Mark's face lowered towards her. His intention was to give her a gentle kiss, something he'd wanted to do since the day he met her. Just get a taste of her. Then their lips touched, the tingling in his limbs ignited and the kiss deepened. He dropped her hand and both his arms came around her, drawing her small form against his solid frame. She felt soft and strong all at once, and despite his encircling arms, she managed to get her own arms up and around his neck, drawing him even closer.

Their tongues found each other and the tingling became fire.

What the hell am I doing? As suddenly as the kiss began, it ended. He drew away, and she fell against the back of the couch.

"I'm sorry. I shouldn't have done that. I ..." he was breathing heavily. So was she.

"Mark, really. There's no need to apologize, I asked for that."

He stood up and held his hands in front of him as if he was warding off the passion.

"No. Really. It wasn't professional. It's not like me."

He blew out his breath, feeling mortified to his toes. How had he let this happen?

But she stood calmly and claimed both his hands this time, squeezing them tightly. Letting him know she shared responsibility for the kiss.

"Look. I know you're attracted to me. Well, I know *I'm* attracted to *you,* at least. Maybe we need to take this slow, but I don't see any reason to ignore the reality here," she said.

He'd been avoiding her eyes, but now delved deeply into them. It was true. He could see it. She wanted him as badly as he wanted her. But it was also true that he was investigating the disappearance of her roommate. He shouldn't even be on this "date," much less grabbing her and devouring her mouth.

Mark dropped her hands and paced the room. He needed to cool down, and he wasn't sure how. He had never wanted a girl as much as he wanted this freckle-faced beauty who sat back down on the couch and watched his pacing.

"My clothes are dry by now. Do you want me to call a taxi?" she asked.

He stopped walking and shook his head.

"Of course not. I'm fine now. I brought you here; I'll take you home."

She got up and went into the bathroom, leaving him alone with his melancholy. He wished the case was over or they'd met under different circumstances. He wished the night could continue in the direction he knew both of them wanted it to.

A few minutes later she reappeared in her own clothes, holding the sweats towards him. "Thank your sister for me," she said, not meeting his eyes. *Had she had a moment to regret what had passed between them?*

When they were outside again, they discovered the rain had stopped. Both were silent on the trip back to her house.

She broke the silence. "I'm sorry," she said, her voice small and unsure. "I made you uncomfortable." He looked over to see her staring out her window.

"You have no more reason to be sorry than I do. You did nothing wrong," he said. "I *am* attracted to you; very attracted. I probably shouldn't even admit that. But I'd like to pursue this when we can. It just isn't a good idea while we're working on this investigation."

She turned her head back then and a small smile let him know she liked what he'd said.

They had arrived at the apartment. Mark moved to get out of the car and walk her to the door, but she stopped him with her hand and insisted it wasn't necessary. She hadn't yet opened her own car door.

"You're probably right—and I get it. We shouldn't be dating until this is over. But is there any reason we can't just spend some time together? Is there any harm in getting to know each other? You seem like you could use a friend. I know I can."

He nodded his head, then turned to see a teasing grin on her face, her hand now raised in a girl scout's pledge.

"I promise not to ravish you until this is all over," she said.

He felt a huge pull towards her—a desire to reach over and trace the outlines of her wonderful face, feel the edges of her mouth that were turned up in a smile. He settled for a smile of his own.

But as suddenly as the lightness arrived, darkness descended. Fear and sadness returned to her face.

"And if this all ends badly with Carla, I'll need that friend even more than a lover," she added.

He leaned over and kissed her cheek, willing the lightness to return.

"Let me take you to dinner tomorrow night. You can use the distraction."

"Thank you," she said and got out of the car.

He watched as she walked into her building. She had barely shut the door behind her when his cell phone rang.

"Another disappearance," McCoy's voice cut through the night. "A young boy has gone missing from Culpepper, Virginia."

Mark dialed Sam's number.

CHAPTER TWENTY-FOUR

HE PULLED THE CAR over to the side of the road and glanced into the back seat. "Still asleep," he said as he reached over and pulled the blanket up over the boy's face.

"You shouldn't have run away," he said. "Your mother is upset. Your Maw Maw misses you. She will be so happy to see you. We have a new house I built by myself—in the side of a mountain. It's all brick—no wood at all."

Jamie was no longer sleeping but Mr. Tom didn't need to know it. He'd kept his eyes tightly closed and now tried to peek out from under the blanket, but he couldn't move his arms. Mr. Tom had wound a rope around him and put a rag in his mouth.

He smelled Mr. Tom lighting up a cigarette. The man inhaled deeply and continued his ranting. "Your mother won't let me smoke inside, but I guess I can't blame her. I wish she weren't so afraid of everything though. She shivers when I touch her. She cries way too much. I can't seem to keep her entertained. That shouldn't be a problem with you. I bought us lots of games to play Scrabble and checkers and much more. No more television or video games. We're going back to the way it used to be. We do have electricity, though. I found a generator and fixed it up. Even got your Ma a stove and fridge. Filled it full of food, too, and bought the meat all diced up already. Can't have any sharp knives around. One of you might get hurt. We got good plastic forks—the ones that don't break the minute you use them—and lots of metal spoons. You always ate with a spoon anyhow."

Jamie heard the man yawn; heard him grind out his cigarette. "I'm getting awful sleepy though. Been a long day and this drive in the rain hasn't helped." Jamie felt the car exiting whatever road they were on.

"Got to rest a bit," he said as the car came to a stop. The car door creaked as Mr. Tom got out and came around to his door. He opened it, reached in, and picked up Jamie, blanket and all.

"You'll be safer in the trunk for now," he said as he went around to the back of the car and deposited his bundle on the ground. Jamie heard the man curse, talk about his keys, then walk away. He wiggled and squirmed until he could just see outside the blanket. They appeared to be in an abandoned rest area. No cars, no trucks, just the road ahead and behind. He saw headlights approaching though and tried to summon the strength to yell. But he knew it was useless. The car went by, silhouetting the returning Mr. Tom, who came armed with the bottle and cloth.

He'd seen Jamie's open eyes.

"It's just for an hour or so, buddy boy. Can't take no chances that you'll run away again."

Mr. Tom lowered the cloth towards his face, and Jamie started to struggle. His head thrashed side to side, but it was no use. Mr. Tom and the cloth were too close.

The world started to go black again, but just before he passed out, Jamie visualized what he'd seen in the headlights.

A billboard: Luray Caverns, twenty miles.

CHAPTER TWENTY-FIVE

SAM RUBBED his eyes. He just couldn't sleep, kept up by the four cases of missing people. As a parent who'd lost a child, he knew the pain the families felt. He couldn't fill the holes in their hearts but maybe he could help them find answers.

Despite the fact Richmond, the other police forces and now the FBI were cooperating, no one had been able to find the missing link that would help them connect the crime to the criminal. Mark and the Richmond police were still trying to locate Don Thomas, the second possible birth father for Carla Dunlap. But the first candidate, Peter Grindage, appeared to have had no contact with Carla, even though his sister June had.

Meanwhile, the only strings that tied any of these four people together were a well-known preacher and coffee shops. It really was a puzzle. But then, puzzles were what kept the blood in Sam's veins pumping.

He'd finally gotten out of bed about three a.m. and grabbed the index cards he'd started for each of the people and hung them up on a bulletin board in his home office.

He studied again the background of each victim, puzzling at why a college student, a housewife, an elderly woman in a wheelchair and a small boy would be taken, if indeed they were all snatched by the same person. He took down the index cards, then started putting them up again, starting with the elderly woman at the top, then the housewife, the college student, and the pre-teen boy. He put the copies of each of their pictures beside the index cards.

They were all Caucasian—that might be significant—whoever was doing this may have chosen them for their race. Were they dealing with someone whose past was connected with white suburbia or maybe something more sinister such as white supremacy? Was he snatching them to punish them or save them? Why not snatch them all at once, and why from families with disparate income levels?

The four did had similar coloring as well as skin color. The housewife had brown hair, the college student and pre-teen were lighter-haired—the boy a dirty blond, the student a paler blonde that could have been enhanced by chemicals. The elderly woman had gone white.

The housewife and college student both had rounded lips and cheeks and narrow blue eyes. The body types, however, were not the same. The college student was thin and athletic-looking. The housewife's body had settled into middle age—plumper and full bosomed. The boy's body type didn't resemble either of them, which was understandable given his age. He had the awkward physique of a boy who would soon be a man—limbs that were too long for the rest of his body parts and shoulders that had started to broaden. Yet he was a petite version of what most boys were at twelve years—he could have been eight or nine judging by his size. It wasn't likely this boy would grow into a large man.

Both the housewife and Carla had recently attended the York United Methodist church, and Millie had listened to his show so those three had similar religious background, but the boy's parents didn't even attend church. Surely religion couldn't be the common factor?

Sam sat in his easy chair, going over the facts and lives of each of them and trying to draw a possible line. He finally fell asleep about four-thirty with pictures of them floating in his head.

He dreamed of Davie again, but this time, it was neither the strange dream that involved the car or his usual dream: that horrible moment when Sam realized his son was missing. This time he dreamed of earlier years, when Davie was just a small boy, still in a high chair. He and his first wife Barbara were together. The family sat at the dining room table, which was set for a Thanksgiving meal. The adults were not talking to each other—they'd run out of things to say a long time ago. But they fed the boy his first bites of turkey. He'd spit it out, but loved the dressing and gravy and had it smeared over his face in a short amount of time. He and Barbara had shared a rare laugh together.

At six in the morning, Sam's eyes popped open. "My God!" he exclaimed, jumping out of his chair, "I think I know what this is all about."

Sam went in and kissed Maggie on her cheek. "Going to the office and then on to Richmond," he whispered. "Love you."

"Me, too," she mumbled sleepily, then turned over and went back to sleep.

"You're just the two people I wanted to catch before I head out this morning," Sam said as he spotted the tall, young Danny Jones pushing his wife Casey's wheelchair through the office door.

"Oh, oh," laughed Danny, who wasn't in uniform this morning. "Sounds like Sam has a job for us on my day off. Guess the gutters will have to wait."

"I'm sorry, Danny. I know I'm asking for yet another favor. But this is important and something I think we need to jump on."

"Anything for my favorite detective," Danny said. He sat down on one of two chairs beside Casey's desk. Casey picked up a pad. Both had eager expressions on their faces. Sam loved that look. Like Sam himself, his two protégées and friends loved nothing better than a good puzzle—Casey relished any part of her job that involved research. Danny enjoyed helping Sam because it was a welcome relief from street work and a step closer to what he eventually wanted to do: detective work. It also allowed him to show off for the man that had guided him into law enforcement. The only thing that got Casey and Danny more excited than working on a case was the two miracles they had at home. Despite the fact doctors had once told Casey that children would be difficult for them, the couple had a little boy and an infant girl.

Sam stopped rubbing his tired eyes and studied their faces. He felt blessed to have these two people in his life: not just as his surrogate family, but also as his helpers. They'd become experts at Internet surfing, which for a detective who still used index cards to figure things out, was invaluable. The index cards had led him here, however.

"What's our gig?" Danny prodded.

"I want you to use your impressive computer skills and maybe a phone call or two and find me a man whose entire family was involved in a tragedy of some kind: a car wreck, an explosion, something that may have taken them away. You're searching for someone who may have lost a wife, an older daughter, a young son and a mother or mother-in-law to injury or death. The mother might have been incapacitated by the event or she may have been in a wheelchair before it occurred. You probably need to go back a few years and the geographic area probably should start on the east coast: Pennsylvania, Virginia, Maryland maybe—you may have to expand that, but start with those locations.

"You think this is a nutcase replacing the family he lost?" Danny said. He'd already figured out Sam's line of thinking.

"Or at least something similar," Sam said. "I'll bring my idea up with Mark and his crew when I get to Richmond, but I'd like to be able to give them some possibilities based on what you find. It's a pretty wild idea, but my gut is saying it's right," Sam said.

"Well, we know better than to ignore that gut of yours, Sam," Casey said. "Danny and I will find him. It may take a while, but we'll find him."

"I knew I could count on you two. I'm on my way to Richmond, and I have a feeling we'll head to Culpepper later this morning to talk to police and the family of the latest victim. I may take Mark up on his offer and stay in Richmond tonight. Give me a call on my cell if you find anything."

"You mean *when* we find something," Danny said. Sam grinned at the comment, and the warm feeling he always got around these two bolstered him far more than the cup of coffee he planned to take on the road.

How had he gotten so lucky to have found this second "family"—one who shared his passion for pursuing answers? Danny had gone from homeless to the police academy with a gentle push from Casey and Sam. Casey had been one of Sam's early cases and had evolved into his right-hand assistant as well as his main cheerleader.

How many times had the three of them looked out for each other? They'd become a crime-solving trio.

CHAPTER TWENTY-SIX

Tuesday, November 22

MARK POURED himself a cup of coffee and sat at his kitchen table, letting his thoughts race in several directions. He was pretty sure he'd dreamed of Melissa last night, though he couldn't recall the details. He remembered feeling like she needed his help desperately but some invisible force held him back from reaching her.

He wasn't sure why his mind was so consumed by this woman after only a few weeks of knowing her, but he was glad things had come to a head last night. It felt right to be able to admit he was pulled towards her. And he hoped to get a chance to take things further.

There was much to do before that could be allowed. He needed time to focus on this case—to get somewhere helping Carla and the others. He wasn't sure when it had happened, but he'd developed the hope they were still alive. It wasn't really logical given the statistics. And now, there was a little boy gone missing.

From his studies, he'd learned that serial criminals—those who committed similar crimes on a string of people, usually picked a type. Sometimes they didn't even realize what they were doing; they just acted under whatever driver set them off in the first place.

So why this particular group of people? The man obviously chose the people by visiting coffee shops and other public places to find them.

Or maybe he just liked coffee and park benches, Mark thought, picking up his own cup and taking a sip.

No. If his training had taught him anything, it was that this was a person acting from some inner turmoil—anger, fear, the need to prove himself, sexual perversion. Something was setting him off and setting his course of action.

It could be anything. Mark took another sip and thought about toasting a bagel.

Ah well, I'll treat myself to a donut at the office, he thought. He got up to go to his room and finish getting ready. But as he was passing the large picture window in his living area, his eye caught a blue SUV turning into the driveway.

What the heck was Janet doing here at seven-thirty in the morning? She lived more than twenty minutes away in Ashburn, Virginia.

And hadn't she scheduled another trip to Traverse City over the coming Thanksgiving weekend to finish cleaning out their mother's house? Why would she be coming his way today?

Was there an emergency at home? Why hadn't she called first?

He was even more puzzled and worried when he saw her face. She walked up the walk clutching her purse tightly to her body, and when he opened the door and her eyes came up to seek his face, he saw they were red rimmed as if she'd been crying for a long time.

She walked into his open arms.

"What is it? What's happened. The kids? Ben?"

She said nothing for a moment, just rested her head on his shoulder.

"Everything's fine at home, Mark," she mumbled against his chest.

When she finally pulled back, her face was calmer, as though she'd driven all that way just to get his hug.

"Got a cup of coffee?" she asked.

"Sure. Come on in. I haven't finished this pot. I'm due at the office, but not for a while."

They walked into the kitchen together. He poured her coffee, and they sat together not saying anything for the moment. He knew she'd share what she needed to share on her own time just as he knew the news was not good. He'd rarely seen her without a full regimen of makeup, her hair in place, her clothes carefully selected. Today, she was disheveled, a mixture of wrinkles and redness—even her nose was colored by her emotion. His gut twisted, dreading what it might be that would cause this.

A few sips of coffee later, the words came tumbling out.

"Oh, Mark," she said, her voice almost a whisper. "I'm so sorry. I didn't mean to read it…it should have been you. But I was going through the last of her stuff to get ready for the final trip back and I found it folded up and hidden in the bottom of the old jewelry box where she kept her wedding ring. I read it without thinking."

She opened her handbag and took out an envelope, put it on the table and shoved it towards Mark.

Mark sat for a moment staring at the envelope. He didn't know why, but he didn't want to read what was inside.

Janet leaned forward and patted his forearm.

"It's addressed to you, Mark. I shouldn't have opened it."

Mark put his hand over the one now resting on his forearm.

"That's no reason to be upset. You know I don't care. Why did she write me a letter though?"

Janet just shook her head and withdrew her hand.

Mark picked up the envelope and took out a single sheet of paper. He recognized the stationery. It had been a yearly gift from his father to his mother. She never lost her love of everything paper, and she'd written letters to friends right up until a few weeks before she died.

Dear, dear Mark,

I've never had the nerve to tell you, but I don't feel it's right not to try. It's not likely that either your father or me will get into Heaven after what we've done, but I feel like I at least owe you an explanation.

You see my dear Mark, you're not our child. I know we've made many jokes about you being adopted, but that's not the case either. I'd give any-thing if either of those things were true, but they're not. We stole you. We have deluded ourselves all these years that it was meant to be, but we both know deep down that's not true.

Mark's eyes rose to his sister, his mouth dropping open.

She bowed her head probably to hide the tears he saw in her eyes. Mark continued reading.

Let me explain as best I can. Your dad and I had been married about five years. We desperately wanted to have a child but I couldn't seem to get pregnant. We discussed artificial insemination, but I had a close friend who'd gone through the medical procedure for years with no happy results. We prob-ably would have adopted eventually.

Then providence intervened—or so we told ourselves. We were getting ready to move to a new state, leaving Pennsylvania for Michigan, and I went to the mall trying to forget the empty house we had to say goodbye to that evening when it was time to start our journey. I was used to my house. I was used to my friends. The thought of leaving our home behind along with the people we'd met in our time as husband and wife had me feeling lost. I left your dad at home packing up a few remaining items because I just couldn't take any more sadness. I was looking for a distraction.

After a couple of hours of wandering the mall, I felt guilty and tired of walking around aimlessly, aware that I couldn't really buy anything because it would just need to be packed. I went out to my red Saab in the parking lot, got in and drove home.

You dad was done with what he needed to do and ready to hit the road, so we threw our overnight suitcase in the back seat of the car and left.

The next part of my story will be hard to believe – but it is true, Mark. I swear it is the truth.

An hour and a half into our journey, we both heard a pounding and thought we were having car trouble. It was coming from the rear of the car. We pulled over at a rest area and got out to investigate.

John opened the trunk and we both received the greatest shock of our lives. There, nestled in a blanket, was a child of four or five, maybe six. One foot had broken free of the bundle and was probably pounding on the trunk lid.

That's how you came into our life, Mark. A child stuffed into our car trunk.

At the time, it seemed like a miracle. We were on our way to a brand new life and there you were, already a passenger in the family car.

I picked you up in my arms, tended your bleeding head and fell completely in love. You didn't seem to know who you were or where you were. You didn't even know your own name. You weren't hurt, just confused. You wouldn't even talk to us or maybe you couldn't.

We knew we needed to call the police, but it was twenty years ago. We didn't have a cell phone—our house phone was already cut off.

We got back into the car with you wrapped up in that blanket and half asleep in the back seat and started driving, discussing where we should go; what we should do. And somehow, Mark, we continued driving.

I just couldn't stand the thought of turning you over to social services to be given to a foster family. I think we convinced ourselves on the way to our new home that we'd take you in temporarily until we could find out what we needed to do. But somehow, we just never did it. We couldn't. Our greatest fear during those first few weeks was that you'd suddenly remember I was not "Mom" and he was not your "Dad," but it never happened.

We really felt you were meant to find us—be rescued by us. Someone had abandoned you by stuffing you into our trunk—we were pretty sure you couldn't have fallen in because I had a bad habit of not locking the car, but I wouldn't have left the trunk open. In our heads, someone didn't want you. We wanted you. Just as we always have, dear Mark. Enough to convince your uncle to counterfeit some papers to get us by all these years.

I know what we did was wrong – very wrong. And it is wrong of me to ask for understanding. Our only excuse is that we loved you from the moment we set eyes on you. In our hearts, you were our son.

I am leaving you this letter in case you would like to look up your biological parents. I'm not sure when I'll have the courage to give this to you, but I figure if we both pass on, someone will at least find this letter among my possessions.

I won't ask for forgiveness – that would mean we were sorry and there hasn't been a minute when we weren't glad that you came into our life. We loved you every bit as much as Janet and Bill – maybe, in some ways, more because you were such a gift.

Love to you always. And I will always be:
Your Mom

The letter fell out of Mark's hands and fluttered silently to the floor. He stood, not seeming to notice.

His mind couldn't wrap itself around the information the letter had relayed.

"Mark," his sister said quietly, shaking his shoulder lightly. He didn't respond. She pushed harder on the shoulder, causing his head to snap around to her.

"Mark," she repeated, "Come out of it. You're scaring me."

His gaze focused on her face, but didn't make it to her eyes. Finally, he sat down on a chair, put both palms over his face and sighed deeply.

"Are you all right?" Janet asked anxiously.

He shook his head and ran his palms up the length of his head from chin to forward and over his hair. "As much as I always wondered why I didn't resemble you; as much as you two teased about me being adopted—this is a shock." He finally caught her eyes. "It certainly explains the lack of baby pictures and why I couldn't find a birth certificate. The one I used to get my social security and my driver's license was a fake." He tried to smile; the result was a grimace.

"Please don't let it hurt you so," she begged. "I know they meant the best for you."

"It's not hurt," he said. "Just shock. And numbness. I don't even know what to do with this information. My life feels false."

"You're still our brother," she tried to reassure him. "Always our brother. We love you. Mom and Dad loved you."

He sought out her concerned eyes and nodded his head slowly. "I know," he told her. "I know. But kidnapped? Here I am, working on four kidnapping cases as a law enforcement officer. And I was taken away, too. Where are my real parents? Why would they stuff me in a trunk? Why wouldn't I remember them? What is the department going to say when they learn I'm not who they think I am?"

CHAPTER TWENTY-SEVEN

IT WAS ALMOST ELEVEN before Mark got to work that day. He'd called in to explain that a family emergency had occurred, then sat talking to Janet for two hours. Finally, knowing that Sam was probably already at the office waiting on him and that the cases he was working on were too important to allow himself time to wallow in his uncertainty, he dragged himself into the office.

What had happened in the past had to remain in the past for now, though he intended to pursue it. The current cases needed to take priority even though his brain was foggy with confused emotions. For the first time he could ever remember, he didn't want to go to work. He wanted to climb into a hole and figure out how he felt rather than face the office.

Finally, at ten-thirty, he told Janet to go home, splashed water on his face and stared at the man in the mirror, feeling like he'd aged twenty years in just the time it took to read the letter.

Sam sensed the turmoil in Mark the moment he saw the stooped shoulders and disheveled hair. The young man was usually "put together," as Sam called it, even the few times he'd seen him early in the morning. Today, he looked like he'd just rolled out of bed despite the fact he was late getting into his office.

"Not feeling well?" he prodded.

Mark plopped down at his desk and ran his fingers through his messy hair, trying to tame it. "I'm okay."

"Is it this case?" Sam asked as he sat down opposite the younger man. "Is it keeping you up at night? I know I had a rough one last night. But I have a few ideas I want to run by you."

Mark's eyes suddenly focused on Sam, and an eager look replaced the vacancy that had been there a moment ago. Sam's mention of the case must have been the lifeline the younger man needed.

"I slept okay. It's personal stuff. You have some ideas?"

Sam tried one last time to get Mark to unburden himself.

"Is it anything I can help with?"

Mark straightened in his chair, grabbed his tie, and twisted it into place, aligned a notebook on his desk. "No. Maybe. I don't know. Can we talk about it later maybe? Tell me your ideas on the case."

Sam gave up, reached for a pencil, and began twirling it through his fingers as he talked.

"I think all of us—the FBI, Richmond, the other police departments all know we're dealing with someone who is taking these people for a reason. Someone who's probably mentally ill or an egotist who has created his own little world. We can't seem to get a handle on why they are selected."

He put down the pencil and leaned back in his chair.

"I have a theory. I want to run it by you first before I report it elsewhere."

"Okay."

"Because he's picked different ages, without regard to what else is in their background. Because one is an elementary school kid, one a housewife, one a college student, one an elderly person, I think he is building himself a group of people: My theory is that they looked just enough alike, maybe he's building a new family. I have Casey and Danny looking into it."

Mark leaned back in his chair, and Sam could see that whatever had been troubling him was replaced by wheels turning in his brain. Mark was mulling over the theory.

After a few minutes, he smiled crookedly.

"It makes sense, Sam. And I like the fact that if it's true, they may still be alive. I'll pass your idea on to the task force and let the others think about that angle as well. I have a conference call with them at eleven-thirty."

"But after that is a trip to Culpepper, and I'm hoping you'll tag along as usual. We need to interview the boy's parents, and get our own impressions of what they've told the police. Can you be ready in forty-five minutes?"

"Of course," Sam said.

The two of them didn't leave, however, for another hour and a half. When Mark finished with the task force conference call, he had some information he wanted to share with Sam and his boss. The private eye wasn't an official member of the task force—it was made up of reps from the various police departments along with the FBI. But Mark fully intended to keep Sam close to his side to see this through. Both of them had been involved since Carla Dunlap disappeared, and he'd come to respect Sam's brain. He liked the new theory, and he ushered Sam into his boss Bob McCoy's office to relay the information he'd just learned and talk about what Sam had come up with.

"They located the second possible 'dad,'" Mark said.

"Don Thomas?" Sam asked.

"Yes. Mr. Thomas is, indeed, the man listed on Linked In who works for Smith and Wythe, which has an office in Richmond."

"But he works for the Phoenix office, right?" Bob asked.

"That's the thing. Yeah, he's in Phoenix for much of his time: the police are on their way to his house there hoping to interview him and his wife and maybe bring him in for additional questioning.”

“Really? Do they consider him a person of interest?” Sam asked.

“Yes, and here’s why: he’s been spending more and more of his time each month here in the Richmond area, according to the jewelry company’s human resources department. His excuse is that he’s brought in a few major accounts in the area and he’s getting them set up for the east coast office to handle. We won’t know until we touch base with him directly if he’s been in touch with Carla or Carla’s been in touch with him, but it’s worth pursuing.”

“Here’s what really odd, though,” he added. “We’ve been calling his cell ever since we made the link and affirmed his identity. Thomas lists that cell as his work number. He doesn’t seem to have a home phone in Phoenix or an office land line in either Phoenix or Richmond. His office has also tried to locate him. He’s not answering the cell. Neither office knows where he is!”

“Well that makes life interesting,” Bob said.

On the way to Culpepper, Sam decided to test again if Mark wanted to talk about what had been troubling him that morning. He took a stab at what he thought it might be.

“How are things between you and Melissa?”

Mark glanced at Sam, surprise lighting his eyes.

"What are you talking about, Sam?"

Sam chuckled softly and turned to face the scenery whizzing by. He was smiling when he brought his gaze back to Mark's face.

"It's pretty clear to me you're smitten with that petite fire bomb," he said.

"But how did you know we went out?" Mark said, concentrating on the road.

"I didn't. So … how did it go?"

"It wasn't exactly a date, Sam. She was going to take me out to dinner to thank me for going along to York, but we ended up at my place."

"Oh?"

Mark took his eyes off the road long enough to narrow them at his companion.

"It's nothing like that, Sam. It was an innocent dinner. We got caught in the rain and dried off at my place." His eyes went back to the road.

"But we did acknowledge an interest in each other," he added.

"Oh?" Sam repeated.

"That is *so* not what's bothering me Sam. Melissa and I know we can't pursue it right now. But that doesn't mean we can't get to know each other. We're supposed to go to dinner tonight."

"Oh." Sam said one last time.

The next twenty minutes the two men didn't talk. Mark's mind was whirring, wavering between his own troubles and the case. Finally, he decided it might help to share the part Sam knew nothing about. He really could use some input on what he should do about his birth, and he trusted Sam's discretion; he wasn't ready to confess to his own boss and the police force that he probably had given them a false background.

"I have a mystery of my own," he said. "Maybe when Casey and Danny are done with this assignment they can help me figure this one out."

He began to explain what Janet had unloaded on him.

It was almost two when Mark and Sam were greeted at the door of Jamie White's home by a tall, slim man with scholarly glasses that magnified the distress in his eyes.

Jamie's father—Philip White—and his mother Fran White—were both high-ranking corporate executives. Fran was almost as tall and thin as her husband with graying hair pulled back tight in a bun at the nape of her neck. Despite what the couple must have been through the last twenty-four hours, the Whites had arisen this morning and dressed in suits like this was just another day in which they'd give orders on how things should be done. They'd probably done so without even thinking about it.

Their demeanor ruined the in-charge look, however. Despite the too stiff posture, Sam wasn't fooled. He could probably knock either of them over with a hearty breath right now.

They were in shock.

"We don't understand," Philip said. "Why haven't we received a ransom note?"

"We have some ideas," was all Mark offered. "Can you tell us a little about what kind of boy Jamie is?"

"Jamie is such a smart boy," Fran said. Her voice broke and she gasped, unable to go on. Philip grabbed her hand.

"We just can't believe he might get into someone's car and let them take him away. We've warned him and warned him about it!"

"He looks small," Philip piped in. "That's the Celiac he had as a boy. We didn't discover he was allergic to gluten until he was about five and some damage had been done. But he isn't a weak kid; he thinks on his feet. He's the brightest child in his class, near genius last time we tested him out."

"Does he have any close friends that might give us some information?" Mark asked.

"Not at school, I don't think. He's somewhat of a loner there. He has a lot of online friends, though, and he texts a lot of them. He's constantly on that cell phone."

Mark and Sam exchanged a look.

"And what do these online and text friends say?"

"The police took his computer and I believe they're contacting those with emails and those linked to games. Nobody heard from him after yesterday morning," Philip said. He was flexing his fingers as though they'd been cramping up.

He's probably been wringing his hands, Sam thought.

"What about his phone and those text friends? They hear anything from him?" he asked.

The faces of both Philip and Fran crumbled as if their visitors had socked them in the stomach.

"He didn't have it with him. We put him on probation for getting in trouble at school and that was his punishment—we didn't allow him to take it to school," Fran said.

"If he'd had it with him the police would be able to track his location," Philip added.

So that was the reason for the looks on their faces, Sam thought—guilt about the phone.

"If someone took him, he or she probably would have disposed of it anyway," he said, hoping to ease the pain.

Philip nodded his head, but Sam didn't think his reassurance helped much. Being reminded it could be a kidnapping probably wasn't easy on them, either.

"The police have begun talking to his contact list," Philip said. "Jamie texted a couple of them before he left for school that day, but that's it. The last text was at seven-thirty-five. He leaves at about seven-forty to get to school by eight. It had to have happened on the way. When he didn't show up, his teachers alerted the office. We got the automatic call, but neither of us checked our messages until about eleven. We were both in meetings." Philip sounded like he'd rehearsed the lines, but Sam knew it was probably because he'd already had to explain all this several times.

"How had he been lately? Was he angry that he was on punishment for the phone?"

The couple gazed at each other like they were trying to weigh how to answer Sam's question. They shook their heads almost in unison, then both turned to Sam.

"Jamie doesn't generally get angry," Fran said. "He didn't even go through the terrible twos."

"Jamie didn't seem upset," Philip added. "You'd think given the fact he seems so attached to both his computer and phone that he'd at least fight us. But he's been on restriction before—just around here at home. And like my wife said, he's not one prone to anger."

Next up on the list of places the detectives wanted to visit was the home of two elderly sisters, the only potential witnesses to where Jamie went that morning. They'd been sitting on a bench in a park that the boy often traveled through on his way to school. The women lived together in a little bungalow within walking distance of the park and had been taking their morning constitution when they stopped to rest. They'd seen Jamie's face on the news and called the police.

"I can't believe that little boy has gone missing," Mildred Bishop said now.

"And from the very park where we walk every day!" added her sister Audrey. Two gray heads of hair bobbed up and down as the women shared what they knew—disbelief etched on their features.

"I don't think the police know that it was the park for sure. But we've come to talk to you because you called and said you saw him that morning," Mark said.

The ladies looked at each other, then turned towards him.

"Oh, we didn't really know anything about this until the police put out that announcement on the eleven o'clock news. When I saw the picture, I just knew it was him!" Audrey said.

"And you'd seen him there before?" Sam prodded. He'd already read the police report.

"Oh yes. Quite a few mornings," Mildred said. "He'd be walking and looking at his phone. I swear I don't know how the kids do it!"

Mark's head came up from his notebook.

"Did he have cell phone when you saw him yesterday?" Mark asked.

"I don't think so," Mildred said, tilting her head to think. "He just walked up to the bench and sat down next to that man we mentioned."

"They were talking like old friends," Audrey said. "Then it began to drizzle so we had to get up and leave."

"You said the man was nondescript. Do either of you remember anything at all about him?" Sam interjected.

"He was pretty well built, like maybe he was a day laborer or a farmer or something. He wasn't all muscly though—I hate that. But he wasn't all soft either," Audrey said.

Mildred gave her sister a slight jab on the shoulder.

"We weren't close enough to see his muscles, you goof!"

"I notice these things," Audrey retorted. "Even if you don't. We didn't see his face, though. He wore a hoodie.

Mark and Sam exchanged a glance. Didn't Helen's neighbor mention that the supposed funeral director wore a hoodie?

"And the man and boy left together?" Mark asked.

"We don't know that for sure," Mildred said. "I saw the man turn and start walking. The boy reached into his pocket, then seemed to hesitate like what he wanted wasn't there. The man turned back towards him, and the little boy started walking in his direction," Mildred said. "We were standing under our umbrella and walking away by then."

As the two detectives walked back to their car, Sam turned to Mark

"The women said the perp and Jamie were talking like they were old friends. This guy seems to have the ability to get people to trust him. He certainly befriended Helen Perkins easily enough that she agreed to go with him. And Alice Springer trusted him enough to get in his car."

Mark was shaking his head. He was about to add his thoughts when a call came in. He held up a finger and dug out his cell phone, stopped to listen for a few minutes, then said simply: "Interesting."

Hitting the end button, he turned to Sam.

"Well this just got a little more complicated," he said.

"What is it Mark. What have they found out?"

"It seems our Don Thomas is a very busy man. We know he has a wife and home in Arizona. It appears he also has an apartment in Richmond. And another woman claiming to be his wife answered the door. Neither women knew where he was. Guess we know now why he isn't answering his cell phone."

CHAPTER TWENTY-EIGHT

SEEING THE TIRED LINES in Mark's young face, Sam offered to drive back to Richmond.

The younger man leaned back in the passenger seat, sighed heavily, and closed his eyes. Silence filled the car for most of the hour-and-a-half drive.

But Sam sensed the other man's restlessness and when they were almost back to Richmond, he said, "You're not asleep."

"No," Mark said.

"Want to talk about the letter, and what we should do?"

"Not really, Sam. Since you're staying the night, we might do that later. But if you don't mind, let me drop you off at my house so I can take the car. I've got somewhere to go."

"Of course," Sam said, turning down the street that led to Mark's house. He didn't ask where Mark was going because he was pretty sure he knew.

Mark drove too fast getting to Melissa's apartment. He wasn't sure what his urgency was. He wasn't even sure if she was home; he'd called earlier and canceled their planned dinner. What Mark did know was that he needed to talk to his new friend now; no one else could calm him.

Melissa was dressed in yoga pants and a sleeveless t-shirt emblazoned with her school's team logo. Her curls were messy; she wore no makeup and no bra and he couldn't help noticing her nipples outlined in the soft material. Her glasses were perched on the end of her freckled nose indicating he'd probably interrupted her studying. Mark thought she looked adorable.

Her eyes widened when she saw who it was, but she didn't even ask why he'd come. She just welcomed him into her home and offered a cup of tea.

When they were settled on the couch, Mark began.

"This morning my sister drove down from Ashland with a letter she found. It was from my mother, and it had been hidden in her desk."

Melissa sat silently taking small sips and absorbing what he was saying.

"Remember what I told you about not being able to find my birth certificate? The letter explains why. It was a confession; an admission I'm not really her child. My mother and father were not my real parents."

Melissa set her tea on the table.

"You were adopted. That must have been a shock, especially after I just told you about me. I remember how hard it was for me when I was little. Realizing that there might be other parents out there."

She reached out and rested a hand briefly on his shoulder. It fell off as Mark sat back hard against the cushions of the couch, his head falling into his open palms. After a moment, his face came slowly out of his hands, and he turned to face Melissa.

"Believe it or not, Melissa, it wouldn't have been that much of a shock if I'd found out I was adopted. Like I've said, I don't resemble the rest of the family. It's why my siblings always teased me so relentlessly. I guess they had no idea what was really going on."

This time, Melissa leaned towards him and gently laid one of her hands on the back of his. He noticed the bright pink nail gloss. And how warm and soft her palm was.

"What is it, Mark? What's eating at you?"

Mark sighed heavily, then turned his hand over to entwine his fingers with hers. He felt like the skin of her hand melted into his.

"I was kidnapped—by the people I thought were my parents. Here I am working on these cases and I find out in the middle of all this that I was taken."

Mark's grasp tightened. Then he released her hand and covered his face with both palms again. His shoulders began to shake. He tried to stop the tears;

he'd only cried a few times in his life. But he was powerless against the onslaught of emotion that hit him. Losing his mom to a heart attack, then finding out she wasn't even his real mom in the first place. It was just too much.

He felt Melissa scooch towards him on the couch, felt her arms encircle him and experienced the reality that it wasn't just her hands that were warm. Her whole body; her whole existence was like a soft blanket. She rested her head on his shoulder and suddenly he didn't feel alone with the nightmare of this morning's revelation.

He straightened his shoulders and sat up, bolstered and ready to talk. Melissa scooted back a few feet to give his words and his thoughts room.

"Your parents kidnapped you," she prodded.

"Not intentionally, I guess. Mom claimed it wasn't planned. She'd been at the mall killing time while Dad finished packing for a move they were making that day to Michigan. She picked up my dad, who had waited for the moving van, then they took off for the new home. I was apparently in the trunk, which they didn't find out until an hour or so into the trip when I thumped the trunk lid with my foot."

Melissa's lips scrunched inward, then puffed out as she absorbed this piece of news. She scratched her head.

"Someone left you in the trunk of your mom's car?"

"That's about the gist of it. I was too little to have figured out how to open a trunk and crawl in so it wasn't an accident. I must have been out of it when she drove away from the mall because I didn't wake up for an hour or so. Why someone chose that particular car; how they knew my mom never locked her car; all of that is just one huge mystery."

"And they didn't report this to the police?"

Mark shook his head, the movement slight, his eyes intent on their hands.

"That part isn't quite so mysterious to me. My parents were childless and having troubles conceiving. They were also very good at fooling themselves about certain things. They were wonderful people, Melissa. Don't get me wrong. But I am beginning to understand how this could happen to them. They justified keeping me for a little while to keep me safe; that little while turned into days, then weeks, during which they fell in love with me and couldn't let me go. I don't mean to sound conceited. Maybe it could have been any kid. And it doesn't forgive them for what they did."

He raised his eyes to see Melissa bringing a pointer finger up to rub her bottom lip, a gesture Mark was already associating with her brain analyzing what was happening.

"But what about your real parents? How could your mom and dad live with themselves knowing someone might be missing you?"

Mark reached over and picked up his tea. He took a small sip and grimaced at how cold it now was. Yet the tea tasted right somehow, and he sipped some more.

"My parents were pretty masterful at not facing pain. They had a talent, when faced with the few hardships we faced, at ignoring what was happening and pasting on smiles. I bet they never even discussed what might be happening to the people or person who gave me up or lost me."

"Wow." Melissa said. "Wow."

"I think in those early days, they just figured someone had to have abandoned me on purpose … that maybe it was destiny."

The two were silent for a few moments, letting the reality of what Mark's parents had done gel. Melissa finally broke the quiet.

"What are you going to do?"

"I don't know. I really don't know. As far as I can tell, they managed to get away with it. I certainly can't see dragging their names through the mud at this point. They're both dead and gone. What's the point?"

"What about your job?" Melissa said.

"I know I need to address this with my new boss. But I don't know him yet. I'm not sure how he'll react, and I'm not sure I'm ready to face the consequences of my parents' action. I don't want my boss to pull me off this case."

She leaned back over towards him and kissed his cheek and suddenly Mark wished it weren't just his cheek—that she'd grab him and kiss away his heavy heart.

"This is obviously a complicated situation, Mark," Melissa said. "You know you need to let people know, but I think you need to take it on your own terms. Since you're the lead investigator from Richmond, you may need to at least notify your boss."

Mark put down his cold tea and sought out the warmth of her hand again. He sat stroking it with a finger, longing for the feel of her lips, even if it was just another smooch on the cheek.

"That's a valid point. But my parents managed to hide this for twenty-six years—I don't know how it would suddenly come up. I think I can keep it to myself for a little while yet. I've told Sam, that detective I'm working with from Lancaster. He's promised to help me look into what happened. Come to think of it, he and my boss have a past; they were on the same police force way back when."

"Sam can give you insight, then, on how to approach this. You just need to work it out within yourself how much you want to know," Melissa said.

Mark studied her face. Her brows were raised, her forehead wrinkled with concern.

Yes, I'm attracted to her red hair, her small body, her quick wit, even her mannerisms and especially her intelligence. But it's more than that. She's someone who really cares, and she's not afraid or ashamed to be taking on someone else's worry.

He pulled on her hand and brought her closer so that he could claim the lips he so desired.

Two hours later, Mark was back in his own living room, sharing a late-night whiskey with Sam. Though they both had to get up in the morning, they agreed a nip might help them sleep. They spent fifteen minutes discussing their impressions of Jamie from what they'd learned from the parents.

"He doesn't seem like the kind of kid who'd get into the car with just anyone or go running off in search of adventure and get into trouble," Mark said.

"I agree. I think that, once again, our perp somehow wormed his way into making this snatching a smooth process. I think Jamie knew him, and I think he was chosen."

As the talk died down and the yawns began, Mark switched gears. "Can I ask a question, Sam?" Mark said.

Sam finished his whiskey and sat holding his glass and savoring the smoky flavor the alcohol left in his mouth. He swallowed.

"I think you already know you can ask me just about anything, Mark."

Mark chuckled.

"Yes, I guess I do. Between you and Melissa, I feel I gained two new friends along with this case. I just wanted to get your impressions of how Captain

McCoy will act once I let him know about what I've discovered about myself. I'm almost afraid to tell him right now, with this pending case."

Sam didn't answer right away, and Mark could tell he'd launched a question that was not as simple as he thought.

"Sam?" he prodded.

Sam reached over and set his glass on the table. He seemed to consider for a moment what to say, then must have decided. Leaning back, he began.

"When you told me about what your sister revealed, I wondered if I should bring this up. We were embroiled in what was happening to you so I didn't say anything at the time."

Sam's voice was low and even as if gathering steam to go on to something difficult for him to discuss. He sighed once and ran a hand over his hair.

"The reason it's so hard for me to work on kidnapping cases, why I didn't even want to take Maggie's case when Jenna was taken is that my own son Davie disappeared more than twenty years ago."

Mark felt the breath go out of his lungs. *My god!*

There were not many revelations Sam could have made that would have shocked him more at the moment. Sam's *son*? Another kidnapping situation? How could this be?

Sam scrubbed his tired face with both hands, and Mark realized how exhausted the detective was. He saw the dark shadows under Sam's eyes.

"I'll fill you in on some of the details once we've both had some sleep," Sam said. "But basically, we were shopping together and I got distracted talking to a store clerk about payment. One minute Davie was beside me; the next, he was gone."

Sam looked over at him and Mark felt the age difference for the first time. He could see the tragedy as if it was etched on Sam's soul as well as in the lines of his face.

"It's the one case I never even had a lead on; never found out what happened. It broke up my marriage; it cost me my job."

Mark's little nip of whiskey was threatening to come up on him.

"Sam, I don't know what to say. As confused and angry as I am about the letter, this is worse. It's much worse. I really never knew what was happening to me. I grew up thinking I was a loved kid."

Sam shook his head.

"Don't do that to yourself. This was so many years ago. I'm just bringing it up because you need to know you're not the only one of us that might have cause to excuse himself from this investigation. I told myself after Davie that I'd never get involved with such cases again, especially if a child was involved. But when Maggie came along and asked for my help finding Jenna, I just couldn't say no. And well look where I'd be if I hadn't taken that case. We can talk about this later…I'm ready for bed. I just thought you needed to know."

He sighed then and his face calmed. Mark realized Sam had made what peace he could with what had happened—Davie's tragic unsolved snatching and the happy story of Jenna's rescue. Mark stood and stretched, also ready for bed, but Sam laid a hand on his wrist to get his attention.

"I'm also telling you because I knew Bob McCoy during both those cases. I didn't lose his friendship back in the days when Davie's disappearance sent me in a tailspin, and I got only encouragement in my quest to find Jenna. He's given me nothing but support both times. He can handle your news."

Sam rose then as well. The conversation could go nowhere from there; the two talkers were just too tired. They both had much to do tomorrow, especially given the fact it was the day before Thanksgiving. Sam had hoped to go home tomorrow night so he could share turkey with Maggie. Mark's only plans were a frozen dinner and a ballgame since Janet was going to Michigan. They both now doubted they'd make it home at all.

But despite the whiskey, the weariness, and the impending holiday, neither fell asleep for a while.

Wednesday, Nov. 23

The next morning, after a yawn-filled car ride and two mugs of coffee each, Sam and Mark sat across from each other at Mark's desk bringing their notes up to date. Mark typed at his computer. Sam preferred his notebook and index cards.

Sam's scribbles were interrupted by a distinctive cell phone ring—a fox hunt. That would be Danny.

"Whatcha got?" he said into the phone.

He listened for a few minutes, saying nothing—just nodding his head. The beginnings of a smile formed about halfway through the "uh huhs." "That's great work, Danny," he finally said.

Mark had been tossing side glances his way. He swiveled his chair away from the monitor.

"What?" he said. "What is it?"

"I think we may have him," Sam said.

"Have who?"

"The person who may be responsible for making these people disappear. We don't know where he is, but I believe we may have an idea *who* he could be."

Mark leaned back in his chair now fully focused.

"Well?"

"Danny and Casey discovered that about eight years ago a man named Henry Thomas Evans lost his entire family in a house fire here in Richmond. He wasn't home at the time of the fire; he wasn't responsible for setting it—the fire marshal blamed faulty wiring. But Henry went berserk, he literally had to be carted away from the scene of the fire, and he went screaming and kicking the firefighters and EMS crew at the scene. They kept him overnight in a hospital environment, and then the seventy-two hours required for observation, but he didn't come out of it on his own.

"He ended up in a mental institution, the Chippenwham Mental Health Hospital. When Danny and Casey tried to track Evans down there, they discovered he managed to walk away from the facility a little over a year ago."

"And you think he's our perp *because* …?" Mark asked.

"Because the family included his mother, his wife, his older teenage daughter, and a son of about eight," Sam said. Sam rose from his chair.

"Let's report to the task force what we have. This may mean people need to put off tomorrow's Thanksgiving plans."

CHAPTER TWENTY-NINE

THE CHIPPENWHAM Mental Health Hospital did not look like a hospital or a stereotypical fortified building where people with deep and dangerous mental conditions might be locked away. Sam and Mark drove right up to the front door, which was under an awning, and walked through the door to a brightly lit reception area. The inside also didn't fit the institutional image—it resembled a dormitory waiting room. Bright fall foliage and squash painted gold spilled from a cornucopia on a coffee table. Turkeys and pilgrims adorned the walls. The staff had decorated for tomorrow's Thanksgiving holiday.

"Can I help you?" an attractive, crisply dressed receptionist asked the detectives.

"We're here to talk to Dr. Stephen Whitman about one of his patients," Mark said.

"Dr. Whitman is in this morning, but he's not going to share information about a patient."

Mark flashed his badge.

"I see," the receptionist said. She turned away and spoke into the phone in tones too soft for the detectives to hear.

Dr. Whitman was a balding, sixty-year old, with a small frame, a friendly expression and firm handshake. Mark explained why they were there.

"Yes, your office called. Sorry I didn't have time to alert the receptionist. But come, we'll go to the conference room and I'll share what I can. Would you like some coffee?"

"Coffee would be great. This shouldn't take too long," Mark said.

They traveled to the conference room via a coffee stand, set up in the hallway.

"For some reason, our patients love having coffee available to them twenty-four hours a day," Dr. Whitman commented. "It's decaf after two p.m., but the high-test is out right now," he added.

The trio sat at a long conference table in a small boxy room. Unlike the front of the building or the reception area, the room's furnishings looked used and tired.

"So … Henry Evans," Dr. Whitman said, smoothing down his tie. His bespectacled eyes took in first Mark, then Sam. He sat back and let out a small sigh.

"I'm sorry to hear from the police that this guy may be endangering people."

"Why is that?" Mark asked. Dr. Whitman turned to him.

"As I'm sure you've discovered, Henry lost his entire family in the type of tragedy that, fortunately, few people have to go through—the fire your staff referenced."

"He was vocal and violent when police brought him in and after the seventy-two-hour mandatory waiting period, became almost catatonic. There wasn't much question from the judge whether he needed to be admitted."

Sam leaned forward in his chair, which drew Dr. Whitman's eyes.

"But this surprises you—that he could have possibly kidnapped or harmed people?" Sam said.

"It took a long time and a lot of treatment. But gradually, over the years, he came out of the hole he was in and seemed to come to grips with the fact he needed to go on."

"Really?" Mark asked. He couldn't help adding. "How does anyone *ever* come to grips with something so terrible."

The doctor took off his glasses and massaged the bridge of his nose.

"Maybe 'come to grips' isn't the right term. But once he came out of the nearly comatose, violent state and started to talk, his disposition changed. He didn't always make sense at first, but he seemed to be always planning."

The glasses went back on.

"He liked to keep a pad of paper close to him and draw up what we eventually discovered were construction plans. I believe Henry had a background in drafting that began in the days when it wasn't all done on computers. In the last few years, he also started talking about the future instead of the past."

"And what was the future, according to Henry Evans?" Sam asked.

Dr. Whitman put his chin in his hand and thought for a moment.

"I can't share with you exactly what he said to me, but the gist of what he focused on in group was family, work, routine, living outside these walls."

"So, you think he could have been successfully treated and released?" Sam asked.

The doctor's face clouded.

"I would not render such an opinion, and it doesn't matter, does it? We won't know since he was gone before we could get to that point."

"How did he manage to get out of here?" Mark asked.

"The corporation who owns this facility and set up its security launched an investigation after the incident. He had been transferred from the more secure facility to this place a year before it happened since he was no longer considered a threat. This place has its own layer of security—cameras, locks, etc., but there are several places of vulnerability—places where the cameras don't point. And he still managed to get by the locks."

He shook his head slowly.

"He must have planned it carefully."

Mark tapped the table with his pen, thinking about what to say.

"Doctor. I know you can't give us specifics or let us go through your files without a court order, but do you remember anything about the last few sessions that might help us? Anything that he might have said or done to indicate what his plans were? Or where he might have gone?"

The doctor sat back and crossed his arms, thinking about what Mark had said and probably what *he* could say. He rubbed his chin.

"Not necessarily in the last session or even the last few group sessions. What I can remember is that several times he went off on a tangent: he seemed obsessed with building a fortress. I think that's what he'd been drawing on the pads for years. He didn't talk about it often, but when he did, he seemed passionate."

The doctor made eye contact first with Mark, then Sam.

"I guess it must have sprung from what happened to his family," he said.

CHAPTER THIRTY

JAMIE KNEW that he had to do something to help them all. He was the only one the man seemed to trust not to be confined all the time, and Jamie suspected it was because he thought Jamie was younger than he really was. He didn't discourage that belief, and even tried to act like the small boy Mr. Tom seemed to think he was, playing games with the man as if he didn't understand that he'd been taken, and badgering his kidnapper with questions that mostly went unanswered. Jamie no longer called him Mr. Tom, though. The man insisted Jamie call him Pops.

Pops kept the girl in ropes and the older woman locked in a room. The really old woman didn't need to be restrained. She just sat in her chair in the common room, staring off into space and rarely moving. Jamie knew she was in trouble, but what could he do? Although Pops untied him sometimes to play games, the windows had bars. The door to the outside was locked. Pops had the key.

He'd tried several times to talk to the pretty blonde girl, but Pops cut him off. Said she wasn't a good influence. Jamie didn't bother trying to talk to the older woman in the dirty apron, the one he only saw at dinner time. She moved like she had molasses in her veins, taking a long time for just the simplest tasks like washing dishes or serving the food. Pops watched her every move, but Jamie didn't think it was because he thought she'd escape. He seemed to be waiting for her to come out of her zombie state.

Jamie knew it was up to him to find a way to get out of this. He needed time alone without Pops watching him so that he could get out the cell phone strapped to his leg. And he needed to do it before the battery died or Pops asked him to take a bath or change his clothes.

Pops himself provided him the chance. He'd mentioned football many times in the few days Jamie had been there, talking about how excited he was that they could play catch again. Today, he'd announced in the morning that he was taking "his boy" out for sunshine—the rain had finally let up. He tied a rope around Jamie's waist and led him out the door. Jamie squinted when the first sun he'd seen in two days hit his face. Pops took him to a tree in the front yard, secured the rope to a sturdy tree and took a pigskin out of his jacket.

As they tossed the ball back and forth, Jamie tried to study his surroundings. He was somewhere in the mountains, but he could see no major roads and hear no cars. The house where they were being kept was built right into the side of a hill, like they were all hobbits or something.

After fifteen minutes of catch, Jamie pretended to stumble and fell to the ground. Before the man could reach his side, he reached inside his pants leg and freed the cell, then thrust it into a pile of leaves beside a big rock he knew he'd remember. Now all he needed was time to make a call.

He had to think of a way to be alone for a few minutes.

The opportunity didn't come, but Pops patted him on the back on the way inside, a weird smile spread wide across his face. "We'll do it again son. Tomorrow."

That evening, when Pops went out to buy himself the six-pack he drank most evenings, Jamie dragged his ropes to sit as close to the girl's bedroom door as he could.

"Are you there?" he said to her door.

"Hello, little boy?" the girl said through the door.

"He's gone. I need your help tomorrow."

The pronouncement was met with silence.

"I need your help," Jamie said much louder. *"He's gone for now."*

"Tell me what to do," she said.

CHAPTER THIRTY-ONE

Thursday, November 24

MARK STRODE towards his office Thursday morning, saying hello to the few staff members and officers that had come in today, sacrificing time with their own families to help with this case or fill in on other cases.

As Mark approached his office, his coworker Officer Bailey Myers approached.

"Sam's been called into Captain McCoy's office and said I was to catch you and tell you to get there as soon as you come in."

Feeling hopeful that a positive development had occurred, Mark entered his boss' office. Instead of good news, however, he was met with a pacing captain, who stopped long enough to tell Mark to shut the door.

This couldn't be good. Had they found a body?

"Captain Green of the Lancaster Police called me yesterday afternoon," Bob McCoy said. "He says both you and Sam have used local resources without approval. When I suggested Mark get in touch with you, Sam, I didn't expect you both to interfere with police work in that district. You know how possessive local forces are about data and personnel."

Sam and Mark exchanged a look.

"Do you mean Danny Jones?" Sam asked.

"Of course I mean Danny, Sam. Captain Green says Officer Jones has used police time and local access to general enforcement databases to track down information for you two."

Sam pursed his lips and scratched the top of his head as if he were trying to figure out where this was coming from.

"I don't think Danny would do any of my work on the police department's time, Bob, but yes, we had him track down the information we shared with the task force yesterday, and he may have used department access to databases to find the information. I didn't mean to step on anyone's toes. You know Danny is like family to me; I wouldn't want to get him in trouble. But yes, I've used his expertise. He'll make a damn good detective one day, and I asked him to help Casey research my theory on this case."

Captain McCoy's serious façade dropped completely, and he grinned. "Yeah. I figured as much. Look, I promised Captain Green I would give you holy hell. Mission accomplished. You know how local jurisdictions are, and Danny probably shouldn't be researching stuff at work if, indeed, that's what happened. But what you and Danny learned has certainly made stepping on a few toes worth it. Now, what did the doctor have to say yesterday?"

Mark was just about to outline what he and Sam found out when the door to the office flew open and another police officer burst in. "Sorry to bother you, but you need to hear this." The officer was slightly out of breath.

"What's so important?" Bob asked the arrival. The officer glanced at Sam and Mark, but Bob waved his hand and said, "Go ahead, McGregor, spill the beans."

"I just got off the phone with a twelve-year old-girl in Short Pump who claims she got a text message from Jamie White," McGregor reported. "It says he's being held against his will, and where he thinks he is. It may be a hoax, but we've ask the girl and her parents to come in. They're leaving their Thanksgiving meal behind and heading this way. They'll be here in about twenty minutes."

Ashley Benderson sat between her parents fingering a long braid nervously. Her cell phone lay on the conference table in front of her. Bob and Sam reached for it at the same time, and Bob won the battle. He studied the face then showed it to Sam before gently laying it back down.

"You say you've known Jamie a year?" Bob said.

"We played Cell Fire. Jamie's really good. Then we got to talking by text and well …" Suddenly she seemed small and uncertain about being in this strange place, the focus of attention.

The father broke in.

"We don't know who this Jamie White is, but she says she knows him. She got really upset when this message came in. She says she's pretty sure it's from him."

Bob looked from father to daughter, then used an elbow to straighten in his chair.

"You need to know that Jamie White's cell phone is in evidence. He left it at home, which is in Culpepper, instead of taking it with him to school because he was on restriction," he said.

Ashley's face wrinkled like she was going to cry. Her parents squirmed in their seats. Sam was pretty sure none of them had ever been interviewed by police before, and even though this wasn't an official interrogation room, being questioned by men in uniform was intimidating.

"I know you don't believe me, just like that policeman I told didn't believe me at first," Ashley's small voice said. Then she, too, pushed herself up in her chair as if bolstering her resolve.

"But I know it's Jamie. I know he's in trouble. You have to help him."

The kid has grit, Sam thought.

"Ashley. We appreciate you coming in—I wish there were more responsible kids like you," Bob said, his voice now gentle and soothing. "But do you think it could be another of your friends maybe playing a trick on you?"

Sam, who knew he should probably keep his mouth shut, also knew his friend Bob wouldn't object if he interjected a comment. He was reading the little girl's body language and what he read was that she was scared for her friend, but also somehow felt guilty about something.

"How could he text if he didn't have his phone, Ashley?" he prodded. "Do you know how he could do that? Do you know something that can help the police?"

Ashley glanced over at Sam, probably noticing him for the first time. She was clearly startled by the question, dropping the braid she'd played with.

Since no one had told him to keep still, Sam continued.

"If he's in danger, you need to tell us everything that might help. I promise you won't get in trouble."

Ashley tilted her head as if allowing that piece of data to enter one ear. She straightened and bowed her head slightly at Sam before turning back to Bob.

"Jamie had a big secret his mom didn't know. When she took his phone away, he got a second one. He paid for it out of his own paper route money He got one of those throw-away ones at Wal-Mart and paid at the self-pay machine."

"He's a clever boy," Bob said.

"Yeah, he's pretty smart," she said. "And he was kinda proud he'd fooled everyone—I don't think his teachers ever caught him, and we just kept playing our game at recess times." Ashley dropped her chin to her chest, then, and talked into her lap. "He'd be angry with me for telling, though."

"Ashley, he wouldn't have texted you if he didn't want you to tell us," Mark interjected. "He wasn't afraid of getting in trouble with his mom."

"If this really is Jamie, and not one of your other friends playing a trick, he texted you because he thought you'd have the guts to tell us," Bob added. His words brought Ashley's head up, and, as that idea took hold, she relaxed her shoulders.

"So why are you so certain it's him?" Bob said.

Ashley counted off on her fingers.

"First, because he called me FE for Floppy Ears. He's the only boy who calls me that.

"Second, I'm pretty sure it was the same number he called me from on Sunday night. He got in trouble last week so it wasn't his regular phone."

Sam, Bob and Mark exchanged a look. This was probably good news. If it truly was a phone the boy had used, it likely could be traced, even if it was a burner phone.

Bob picked up Ashley's phone and scrolled with one finger, studying the second half of the message again.

FE: Go 2 police. Kidnapped. 3 women in house built into mountain. Bars on windows. Do NOT send message to this phone. Sign for Luray. Stopped at Hardees. Counted 382 mississippi. Turned right. Counted 2,021 mississippi then gravel road. Will try again tomorrow at 3. If rain, next day.

"Three eighty and two thousand *Mississippi*?" Bob said to no one in particular. "If it *rains?*"

"Wow!" Mark said. "That's quite a kid. The word, "Mississippi" is what kids use to count seconds. Imagine having the foresight to try to show us about where he is by counting. If it rains must have something to do with the outside or where they're located or where he'll be at three."

The Richmond staff's technical crew had been called in. They now had a cell phone number to work with and were trying to pinpoint where the phone last pinged and be set up to get a better location when Jamie turned the phone back on the next day at three.

Meanwhile, Richmond police alerted law enforcement in the Luray, Virginia, area and brought them up to date. FBI specialists and Luray officers began looking into property purchased or abandoned in recent years in the mountainous area that surrounds Luray.

Everyone began mapping a circle beginning at the only Hardees in Luray, which was on main street, to see if they could narrow the search according to Jamie's estimated counts.

Most of the Richmond skeleton crew left what they were working on to help in the effort. All of them, along with Mark and Sam, were working on the premise the little girl had been right: the phone call really was from Jamie.

The people now involved in this case had given up their Thanksgiving Day dinners with one hope: the victims were still alive.

CHAPTER THIRTY-TWO

Friday, November 25

THE NEXT DAY at two, Ashley, her parents and her phone were placed in a conference room also crowded with law enforcement and equipment. While the adults wore serious expressions and bustled about behind computers, tablets, and phones, Ashley chatted away at whoever would listen.

Sam, who was not a telecom expert or an official member of the task force, had little to contribute to the activity in the room. Mark, who sat closest to Ashley, watched the proceedings closely. Both men were targets for the little girl's running commentary on how much she wanted a dog, how much she loved yams with marshmallows, how much she'd missed playing Cell Fire since her phone had been confiscated. When those topics died down, she began throwing questions at Mark about being a policeman and carrying a gun. Mark tried hard to be patient, but Sam could see the tension on his face. For Sam, who was used to his pre-teen daughter Jenna, the prattle was comforting and comfortable. Soon, he had Ashley engaged in conversation so that others in the room could concentrate on what they were doing.

"So, you say Jamie's a brainy kid, huh? He's good at that game?" Sam asked her.

"He's the best. I can never beat him outright, but we've learned to play partners sometimes. I bet he's like *super* smart and he must be like super tall and handsome," she said.

The little girl's light blue eyes sparkled with excitement, and she tossed back her long blond locks in a feminine gesture she would probably perfect as she got older. *I pity those parents; they've got a challenging few years ahead of them,* Sam thought. *And she's got a major crush on little Jamie.*

By three p.m., however, even Ashley had grown quiet, staring at the phone and hoping it would ring or ding.

It was three-thirty before the message from Jamie finally came.

Bring help to house 3 tomorrow if no rain. Will b outside with ball. Women inside safe. Keep quiet. Has guns. Do not call or text.

After the message came in, all hell broke loose. The phone techs reported the time the phone was "on" was too brief to get exact coordinates, but they were triangulating the signal to narrow down the location. Once the team matched that area to data the task force had tracked down on real estate and geography, they used calculations on seconds of travel from the Hardees. A five-acre plot of land owned by a local bank but abandoned for several years was pinpointed as a likely location. The property's closest borderline was three miles out of town in a mountainous area.

The sheriff's office in Page County, which had jurisdiction in the area where the property was located, reported that several dirt and gravel roads led from the main road into the property. The office sent patrolmen to investigate and reported that only one of the roads appeared to be used recently—the rest were overgrown or chained off.

The entire task force was now working with Page County and Luray law enforcement to put together a group that would be part of what they hoped would be a peaceful takedown. Mark, as lead of the task force, and his boss Bob would be part of that group, and they'd approved having Sam along. The three were soon on their way to Luray to join the FBI and the rest of the group.

By the time the sun began to set, officers from the Luray police force and the county sheriff's department had scouted out the property by foot and located what they believed was the "house built into mountain." The only two windows that faced outward had bars on the windows. The officers had been instructed to wait until the arresting force arrived to take any action

CHAPTER THIRTY-THREE

Saturday, November 26

THREE CARS AND SEVERAL STANDBY emergency vehicles left the Luray police headquarters at two the next day to join the officers who had spent a cold night staking out the house in the mountain. Page County Sheriff Jim Gray, his staff and FBI agents were in the lead car of the caravan. Two Luray police officers, a sheriff's deputy, and a local sniper specialist were in the second car. Mark, Sam, and Bob trailed behind that car. The emergency vehicles were last in the progression. Several additional police cruisers would be leaving soon to block the entrance to the other three possible means of vehicular escape: the other dirt roads. There was no need for sirens. The on-site officers watching the house all night reported no activity.

When the caravan vehicles reached the property, they parked outside the gravel drive. The men and one woman in the cars would travel by foot from that spot. The emergency vehicle would wait to be alerted if needed.

"As we discussed this morning, my officers and FBI sharpshooter Purcell will get into position on the west side of the house," Sheriff Gray said. "Chief Andrews, his officer and shooter McGee will come in by the east, which is the best spot for taking a clear shot. Captain McCoy, you and your men come up the gravel road at the south side to ensure the perp doesn't flee that way."

"We know he's armed and dangerous but we believe the message about rain means Jamie will lure the guy out of the house at the designated time," the sheriff continued. "If we're interpreting this right, and the boy is successful, that's our best shot at not harming any of the victims."

"Jamie was clever enough to hide a cell phone and then give us an idea how far out of town they are," Bob interjected. "He may only be twelve, but he thinks like a cop. I have confidence he's figured out a way to be outside at the designated time. Hell, I'm ready to hire the boy."

His comment elicited a few nervous twitters from most of the officers there. However, all expressions turned deadly serious as they tightened their bullet proof vests; checked their weapons and prepared to make the three-quarter mile trek to the site.

Mark, Sam, Bob and FBI Agent Juarez soon lost sight of the men and woman who slinked off into the trees at their right and left. When the four of them could finally see the house in the mountain, they hid themselves behind trees.

The wait wasn't long. At three-twenty-five, they saw a man and a small boy come out of a door at the south side of the structure. The man locked the door behind him and moved into the clearing. Slung over his shoulder was a rope. The boy stumbled along behind him, attached at the waist to the other end of the rope.

The man carried a rifle. He stopped at a large tree in the front yard and put the rifle down long enough to secure the boy to the tree. He pulled the rope tight at the tree and then at the boy's waist as if to ensure himself the boy was going nowhere, then walked away. At about thirty feet from the boy, he turned back and put the rifle down on the ground in front of him. Sam, who was studying the man's face with the binoculars he'd brought, witnessed a transformation at that moment. While their perpetrator had been all business up to this point, he suddenly relaxed, smiled broadly and yelled:

"I'm ready, Son. You ready?" His voice echoing off the mountain sounded almost joyous, which seemed totally out of whack in this tense scenario. But of course, Henry had no idea he was surrounded.

A football came out from under Jamie's arm and he reached back over his shoulder and let it loose. Henry caught it cleanly.

"That's terrific, Tommy. Just great. I think you're getting better!"

Tom, Sam thought. Henry Evan's lost son.

Henry was impressed. He'd only practiced a few days with Tommy and already the boy had greatly improved. He kept falling down, but every time he did, he picked himself right up off the ground and resumed their practice.

Only eight years old and he already had the makings of a quarterback.

It was a beautiful Spring-like day—totally out of season for November—the sun beating down on the home he'd built with his own hands.

His family was finally together again. They still had some things to work out; he didn't understand why his beloved Marjorie was always mad at him. His daughter had caused a few problems, screaming at the top of her lungs right during his practice time with Tommy. But a few slaps was all it took to calm her down, and she'd come around.

This day had begun much differently than the last few, a game of checkers with his now quiet daughter, pancakes from Marjorie. Her mom watching it all from her chair.

Things were back to the way they should be. His family was whole. Tommy's request for more football practice was proof of that. He wanted to learn ball to make his daddy proud.

Henry stretched his back and rubbed behind his head, then circled his throwing arm at the shoulder, preparing for the next toss.

From the corner of his eye, he saw a flash of sunlight on metal and suddenly, his mood crashed. *What was that! Were there strangers on his land?*

He bent to the ground and picked up the rifle. Pointing it where he saw the flash, he yelled, "Someone is out there, Tommy. Get down."

His son fell on his stomach to the ground. *Good boy!* He began walking backward toward Tommy, his rifle aimed at the trees to the east of his house.

"I know you're in there. Come out, or I'll shoot."

From the opposite direction came a voice through a bullhorn.

"Put down the weapon, Mr. Evans. We have you surrounded."

Henry swung 180 degrees and pointed his rifle to the west.

"Lower your weapon and come peacefully, and no one will get hurt," the bullhorn voice said.

Henry swung back to the east, then swiveled around again in the direction of the voice. Sam saw from his binoculars when confusion morphed into fear, then anger. He also witnessed the moment Henry realized he had little choice. He pointed the rifle towards Jamie on the ground.

"Don't make me shoot him," he shouted.

Mark spoke into his walkie talkie to Sheriff Gray, then nudged Bob McCoy and took a second bullhorn. All three groups had the bullhorns, but all had agreed that if the situation permitted, Mark would do the talking based on what he knew and what he and Sam had learned from Dr. Whitman. Mark also had extensive hostage negotiation training.

"We know you don't want to hurt Tommy," Mark said into the horn. "Put down that rifle and we'll see that he's safe."

Henry had reached Jamie and now stood behind him, pointing the rifle toward the road in front of him and Mark's voice. He reached down with his other hand and grabbed the boy's shirt at the scruff, hauling him to his feet and placing him in front of him.

"You're not takin' my family from me. I worked too hard to get 'em back," he shouted at the road.

"We know you care about your family, Henry," Mark said. "We know they were hurt in the fire. The fire wasn't your fault, Henry. We all know that. Let the boy go."

Henry looked briefly in all three directions, his face dark and angry. He held Jamie close to his chest, the rifle still pointed straight ahead.

"Show yourself, mister. Where are you? What do you want with my family?"

Mark made a snap decision. He stepped from behind a tree, holding only the bullhorn. By making himself the focus, he hoped he could keep Henry's attention in one direction. Because he was on the gravel road, in the clear from the trees, he knew Henry could see him.

"Why are you using your son as a shield, Henry?" he said into the bullhorn. "You know you don't want to hurt him. You haven't hurt any of your family. Why would you do that now?" He kept his tone calm and firm.

But Henry had had enough.

"Get the hell off my property," Henry shouted at Mark. *"All of you."*

"We can't do that, Henry." Mark's voice remained even. "You know we can't. Let the boy go before he gets hurt. Don't let your son Tommy get hurt."

Suddenly, Henry's shoulders sagged and the rifle faltered, but he was still clutching Jamie's shirt and holding the boy too close for anyone to take action.

"I can't lose them again. I can't go through this again," Henry's voice was filled with the anguish of thousands of days without his family, thousands of hours of working towards getting them back.

Suddenly, he pushed Jamie away from him to the ground and began walking towards Mark, the rifle pointed directly at him. Before he could fire, two things happened: Sam leaped from his perch on the ground and pushed Mark down, and a shot rang out. It wasn't from Henry's rifle; a sniper had hit his target. Henry slumped to the ground.

Remarkably, Jamie rose from where he'd fallen, but instead of running for safety, he tugged on the rope that bound him, took a few steps, and sat down on the ground beside his captor. He took Henry's head onto his lap. The sniper had chosen to hit the kidnapper at the bigger target: his chest. Blood poured from the wound, spreading quickly across Henry's torso and Jamie.

Mark, Sam and Bob, the closest now to the clearing where the football practice had taken place, reached the boy's side in seconds. Sam could see Henry was not going to make it, though the crew was already on their walkie talkies to the EMS.

"I'm sorry, father," he heard Jamie say to his captor. "Thank you for keeping us safe."

The kidnapper reached a blood-covered hand towards the boy's head as if to smooth his hair. The hand fell to the ground as Henry's chest gave out, and he died.

The boy raised his head and Sam saw tears in his eyes.

"I don't think he would have shot me."

"You're probably right," Sam said as he bent to feel for a pulse. "But he would have shot us, and we couldn't take the chance he'd harm you."

"I guess you're right," the boy whispered. "There was no other way."

He reached into the dead man's pocket and retrieved the key to the fortress built into the mountain.

CHAPTER THIRTY-FOUR

Friday, December 23

"I'M SORRY," Sam said to Mark over the cell. "Maggie and I ran into some engine trouble on the way there. We're probably going to be an hour late. Don't let them hold dinner for us. I think we'll make it in time for the award presentation."

Mark was standing in the hallway of the Culpepper Lions Club. The mayor of Culpepper—Greg Gordon—had invited a group of people to a special dinner and ceremony. The town was honoring its new hero—Jamie White—as well as the others who played a role in saving the kidnapped victims. Everyone connected with the case had been invited—the entire task force as well as the families of the victims. About fifty people had accepted.

Because Mark was lead on the task force and the first case began in his office, Mayor Gordon had asked him to serve as master of ceremonies for a small program and the awards presentation. Mark brought his girlfriend Melissa Burns, who wasn't playacting at being his fiancée this time. There was no media in the room. The press had been invited to the award presentation and to talk to Jamie and others following the dinner.

Returning to the cheerful holiday-decorated dining room from the hallway, Mark put his cell back in his pocket and took his place at the podium. He greeted and welcomed the room full of people, then announced: "Sam Osborne and his family are going to be late—they're having car trouble. Since we all want Sam to be present for the award, I think we'll go ahead with the dinner."

Then, grinning, he added: "Just eat slowly."

When it became apparent the Osbornes would be even later than they'd predicted, Mark decided his few remarks didn't need to wait. Sam and Maggie both knew the intricacies of what had happened—a man driven to insanity after his family died who slipped out of a mental facility and spent a year wandering, ending up in the hills of Virginia, building a fortified home into the side of a mountain. He may have been unstable enough to think he could replace the family he'd lost, but he was intelligent and re-sourceful enough to plan.

His victims were chosen for their physical sim-ilarities to the family he'd lost in a fire caused by an electrical system he himself had installed. Carla had been the first one taken simply because Henry had overheard the conversation about her heritage. He'd used what he learned to lure her. Then he'd gone on to find the other members of his "family."

Mark gathered his notes and went to the podium. He glanced over to see Jamie squirming in his chair, fidgeting with the tie he was probably not used to wearing.

"As you know, we're gathered today to note the heroes of this ordeal," Mark began. "Jamie is receiving an honor today bestowed on him by his hometown of Culpepper." Hearing his name brought a deer-in-the-headlights expression to the boy's face.

"He deserves it," Mark continued. "As young as he was, Jamie started the ball rolling on the rescue efforts. Without his quick thinking, the situation could have been more tragic."

Mark looked around the room and settled his eyes on Helen.

"Helen went almost two weeks without her medications. We're not sure how much longer she could have taken it, if Jamie had not intervened."

Helen's daughter Millie put an arm around her mother and squeezed. Helen glanced over at Jamie and smiled.

Mark sought out Alice Springer's daughter Mary, but decided there was nothing to say. She was brave to have come when her mother had been so traumatized. Her mother and father didn't want to face any more media, and Mary had indicated she'd be slipping out of the proceedings tonight before the press became involved. Mark knew she'd be going home to a mother that would likely be in therapy the longest of any of them.

He glanced next at Carla and her mother Katherine sitting side by side. He was sure they'd spent many nights coming to grips with Katherine's past, as well as Carla's fascination with the preacher, who Mark learned from Melissa had encouraged Carla's advances. Mark also learned from his fiancée that Carla had come to accept the fact George was not her birth father, and the preacher was not in love. Carla's father Don Thomas was sitting in a jail, serving time for bigamy. Despite the fact he already had two families, he'd happily agreed to a paternity test—the man seemed addicted to having children. Meanwhile, the preacher was celebrating his success as a television star, his Teflon smile and personality no worse the wear for the almost-affair with Carla.

Mark smiled at Carla. She'd come a long way.

"Carla was there the longest of those taken, but she managed to keep her head despite how terrified she was," Mark said now. "She tried to help the others, tried repeatedly to get away. And in the end, Jamie and Carla worked together to come up with the plan that took Henry out of that house—which led to the events that allowed us to find them."

His eyes went next to the little girl who sat quietly between her parents, her eyes wide as if fascinated by the whole proceeding.

"Ashley was brave enough to tell her parents, and they believed her and came forward to report what she had to say to the Richmond authorities."

Mark looked to the back of the room, where a table of the people who made up the police task force had settled to swap stories about their various localities. Even FBI Agent Pete Juarez and sharpshooter Amos McGee, who had taken the kill shot, had come.

"I want to thank the various police localities and the FBI, who helped our task force put it all together."

Mark's eyes now swept the entire room.

"Jamie truly is a hero, and I'm glad we're gathered today to recognize what a miracle it is that he found a way to help us track down the location of that house."

"But I'm also glad the rest of us are here because this rescue truly was a team effort. I'm proud to honor Jamie, and I salute the others on my task force who made this happen."

Mark turned the podium over to Mayor Gordon and sat down, accompanied by applause.

When Mayor Gordon was finished lavishing his own praise on those in attendance, he motioned to the officer standing by the door to let the media in for the presentation and a few photos. Mark glanced toward the doorway and saw Sam standing just inside, holding the hand of a little girl that had to be Jenna since she was a smaller version of Sam's wife Maggie. They waved when their eyes connected with Mark, then crossed the room and sat at his table.

"You missed about all of it," Mark whispered.

"Sorry about that," Sam replied, nodding to acknowledge Melissa's presence at Mark's side.

As the cameras and crew poured into the room, Sam took a moment to introduce Maggie to Melissa.

"And this is Carla's roommate, Melissa Burns."

"Oh … Mark's fiancée. Congratulations," Maggie said, grabbing the other girl's hand to admire her diamond.

Sam turned next to Jenna.

"Mark and Melissa. Let me introduce you to my beautiful daughter Jenna. Jenna, this is Melissa and …"

His comments were interrupted by a giggle. Sam's eyebrows shot up.

"Oh, I know who he is," the little girl said, bouncing up and down in her seat. "You're Davie. You found your son, didn't you Daddy Sam?"

Sam's mouth fell open. *How in the world did she come to that conclusion?* He glanced back to see Mark's gaping mouth echoing his: *what the heck?*

"He is Davie, isn't he?" Jenna exclaimed. "Oh, he looks just like you! What a wonderful Christmas present to have found the rest of your family."

Everyone at the round table now turned and stared at the two men.

"You do kinda look alike," Melissa said. She narrowed her eyes as if to focus them better and ran her gaze from face to broad shoulders and back to the face.

Maggie tilted her head. "That's interesting. I remember at the house, after an evening with you, Mark, that something about you seemed familiar. I think it's your mannerisms maybe?" She pressed a finger to her chin and peered even closer.

"Maybe your smile? You both have dimples."

Sam and Mark now studied each other's faces.

Was it possible, Sam thought, calculating the years and realizing that, while they didn't align perfectly, Mark probably didn't know his exact age since his background had been forged.

He felt Mark's eyes boring into him, reading each line and feature of his face. The younger man fell back in his chair with a thud as if absorbing the fact the two hadn't even considered the possibility.

Why would we? Sam thought. Mark hadn't even known his parents had taken him until they were well into this case. Sam hadn't mentioned his own son until a few days before the rescue.

With wrapping up this case forefront in their minds, they hadn't yet started the process of looking into Mark's background.

Suddenly the crowded room faded into the background as the two men locked eyes. Could fate have really entered their lives in such an expansive way? Was this truly a Christmas miracle?

They seemed to realize at the same moment, however, that this was not the time for answers. They were about to start a press briefing, and the mayor had just announced the award to Jamie would be presented. There were DNA tests and investigative tools that could help them seek the answers they wanted.

Sam's attention refocused on Jenna, who was sitting at his other side. He leaned over towards Mark, however, and put his arm around his shoulder. "This gentleman's name is Mark," he said. "But yes, I think he has joined our family."

EPILOGUE

April 26, 2017

DANNY REACHED for Casey's hand and squeezed, seeking strength from this woman he loved to his core. What a journey they'd had—from strangers caught in a snowstorm to best friends, then lovers and now parents. Their lives together had been a twist of fate with a spin neither saw coming: happiness.

It was right that she be here at his side as he made this journey into his past.

Casey withdrew her hand long enough to seek out the slip of paper in her lap pack.

"I think this is it, Danny. 4721 Elderberry Square."

Danny squinted at the numbers on the rusted mailbox attached to the very old brick townhouse. Ivy crawled up the walls of the building, and the window frames needed paint. But the home was sturdy and solid and there were bright red flowers planted in the window boxes.

How many years had Sister Rose lived just a few hours away from him? The nun who'd once taken him in for a week when Gus, his guardian and protector on the streets, had to seek out work to keep them alive for the winter. Danny had not known until he'd begun trying to find her that Sister Rose was truly a sister to Gus, not just the holy woman who'd done them a favor.

That week Danny had spent under her care was his only connection to his past.

"Ready?" he asked Casey.

"Of course," she said. She soothed his nerves with her beautiful Casey smile, and he wheeled her to the street-level door, then rang the bell.

"I can't believe you found me after all these years," Sister Rose's scratchy voice seemed to go with the deep blue veins of her trembling hands, the myriad of wrinkles lining her face and the crackling fire in her light grey eyes.

"I had a little help. Well, actually an entire police department's help." Danny said. He laughed and leaned back in the comfortable old arm chair, taking his tea cup and saucer with him and resting the saucer on his knee.

"Danny just made detective in Lancaster, Pennsylvania, our home town," Casey said. She leaned over the arm of her wheelchair to pat his leg.

"I'm not that surprised, Danny," Sister Rose said. "I only had you less than a week. But I sensed something special and driven in you even then. I had a feeling you'd make it off the streets." She stared into the delicate, gold rimmed tea cup she held, lost in the past.

"I'm sorry I didn't find you and let you know about Gus' passing," Danny said.

She seemed to refocus on the present then and returned the cup to its saucer, spilling a little tea on the coffee table as her shaky hand set it down.

"I couldn't have expected you to, Danny. Gus was his own man. If he'd wanted me to know he was sick, he'd have told me."

She took one hand in the other as if to steady her nerves, then looked at Danny, a question in her eyes.

"But why have you come now? And what it is you need from me?"

Instead of answering, Danny took a moment to study the room, taking in the cross on the wall, the tatted lace doilies on the table, the dozens of photographs. Were these images of people she'd administered to in her seventy-plus as a nun?

He wasn't avoiding her question. He was just trying to frame it right. The answer was complicated.

"I guess you could say I was inspired by a miracle that happened in a good friend's life," he said. "My mentor after Gus was a private investigator, who is now my friend Sam Osborne. He's the one who encouraged me to pursue police work, then this detective's badge. He also helped me find you."

The wrinkles around Sister Rose's eyes smoothed just a little.

"He sounds like a very good friend," she said.

"He is. He truly is."

He fiddled with his cup and saucer to give himself a moment, then put both on the coffee table and straightened his upper body.

"Anyway. Sam's son Davie disappeared two decades ago from a store in the Philly area. Sam was never able to solve the case and it's haunted him all his life."

Sister Rose put a shaky hand to one cheek.

"That's terrible. How sad for him!"

Danny's lips drew up at the corners.

"That's where the miracle comes in. He recently concluded a case working with an investigator within the Richmond police department. You may have even heard about the case: four people gone missing in Virginia?"

"The one where the little boy was a hero?" Sister Rose asked.

Casey chuckled.

"That's the one," she said. "We attended the ceremony where the boy was honored a couple months ago," she said.

"Oh my. I can't believe you were involved in all that!" Sister Rose's voice cracked.

"I was only on the edges of the investigation," Danny said. He ran his hand down the chair's arm, thinking about where to go next with his explanation. He decided to plunge right in.

"As it turns out, the lead investigator in the case turned out to be Sam's son."

"What?" both hands now went to her cheeks and Danny worried for a moment about the shock he was giving this ninety-one-year-old woman.

Casey's laughter drew the nun's eyes her way, and Sister Rose seemed to relax, dropping her hands.

"I know. I know it sounds absolutely crazy, but it really happened," Casey said. "A chance re-mark by a child about how much the two were alike made them both stop to figure it all out. The investi-gator didn't even know he'd been taken as a child un-til he was in the middle of that case."

"But how could he not know?" Sister Rose asked. She glanced from Casey to Danny.

"His parents unwittingly took him," Danny said. "They drove off with him in a car trunk not knowing he was even there. But kept him when they discovered it."

Casey jumped in.

"You see, Sam's child was snatched from a store in the same shopping center where Mark … that's the investigator's name … was abandoned. Be-lieve it or not, police think it was a kidnapping totally screwed up. They think the person or people who took Sam's son tossed him into the wrong trunk— maybe Mark's mom had the same make and model as their car? It's just a theory, but they think the kidnappers were interrupted or went back into the mall or they saw a cop and ran off by foot. We'll never know exactly what happened. And Mark, who began life as Davie, never recovered his memory of Sam or his birth mother."

Sister Rose's hand was to her head as if she had a headache, but Danny was pretty sure it was just incredulousness. He didn't blame her.

She must think we're making this up. But then, how could anyone make something like this up?

Sister Rose's hand came down, and she picked up her tea cup, but set it back down again without taking a drink. She smoothed the fabric of her skirt, adjusted her blouse collar. Danny watched silently, letting her have a moment to take it all in.

Then her weathered eyes sought out Danny's.

"That's quite a tale. Why haven't I read that part of the story in the paper?"

Danny gave her half a smile.

"Sam and Mark managed to keep that piece of information out of the paper. They both needed time to adjust and find out the truth."

Sister Rose nodded her head once in acceptance, and Danny had a sudden memory from his time as a boy with her—he'd come upon a package of communion crackers in the church's storage closet. Curious and hungry, he opened them and took several bites before spitting them out in disgust. Sister Rose had walked in on him mid-spit. Instead of getting mad or yelling at him about defiling a holy ceremony, she'd simply had him help her clean up the mess, then sat down and explained what the crackers and the ceremony represented.

Her voice cut through the memory.

"I guess you have no reason to show up just to entertain an old lady with your tale. But what does this have to do with why you're here?"

Danny ran both hands down his thighs, then placed his palms on his knees.

"I need to know anything you can tell me about *me*," he said. "I need to know where *I* came from."

The old woman's eyes seemed to melt. She rubbed an eyebrow with one finger.

"I'm sorry. I'm not sure what to tell you. There's certainly not a miracle going on there. Gus isn't your father or anything."

Casey reached out then and patted Sister Rose's arm.

"We're not asking for that. But like Mark and Sam, Danny needs to make a connection with his past. Can you tell us anything about when he was a child? How he ended up on the streets with Gus?"

The nun stared at the place where Casey had touched her, then raised her eyes and gave Casey a small smile. She picked up her tea cup and sat back in her chair. Danny could see she was wasn't sure what to say—was she afraid of telling him the truth?

But suddenly her demeanor changed. She sighed and put the tea cup back in its saucer, then used her elbows on her armrests to draw herself up. She clasped her hands and rested them on her stomach, then turned her face towards Danny.

"Gus wasn't just looking for work when he left you with me." She raised a shaky hand to her lips, then ran thumb and forefinger around the bottom lip, which seemed to steady the hand.

"I don't know how he did it exactly, but he found the boarding school where you ended up after your parents died. It was not that far from where he found you, and I don't know … he thought maybe somehow you were trying to get back there—though you were so young, just six or so when he found you."

"My parents." Danny said. He felt the weight of those two words. *He had two parents he'd never known. But if they'd both died, did that mean they hadn't abandoned him as he always assumed?*

The nun's crackly voice interrupted his thoughts.

"I don't know what the circumstances of their death were, Danny, except that it was a car accident. You were dropped off at a boarding school by a man who said he was your distant relative, that he couldn't care for a young child. The school called social services when it happened, but the guy slipped away before they arrived, and you ended up in foster care. He never even left a name, much less the name of your parents."

Danny said nothing. He just sat, his hands now clenched together. His eyes wide. His mouth drawn tight.

"I'm sorry," Sister Rose said again. "I know it's not much. I'm sure the state may have tried to locate your parents, but without even a name, they'd couldn't do much. I don't know how Gus even managed to find out as much as he did. I wish I knew more. I wish I could help."

The sadness Danny always carried on his shoulders—the profound hole in his life left by having no beginning—suddenly got heavier. Only finding Casey and love, connecting with Sam had been able to lighten that burden and give his life meaning.

But that wasn't true, was it?

Suddenly, Danny sat up straighter. In his mind, he flung off his imaginary burden. He unclasped his hands and swiped his brow with one of his palms.

"What happened with Gus?" he said.

"Excuse me?" Sister Rose asked.

"Gus is my roots—*that's* what I really need to know. I wouldn't be alive, I wouldn't be here if Gus hadn't kept me safe and taught me how to live. I need to know how Gus ended up on the streets."

"Oh," Sister Rose said, her eyes suddenly troubled. Her wrinkled eyelids blinked a few times, and she leaned her head back against the chair. When she brought her head back up, she opened those eyes and connected with Danny. But he didn't sense sadness in their depths.

"As I said, Gus was his own man. He would not want you to feel sorry for him."

Danny nodded his head just once.

She smiled then and her entire body seemed to relax into her chair and her story.

"He was a lawyer, then a judge, always a philosopher—since the time he was a little boy. He was constantly trying to figure out how and why things happen. He really loved the law and got a degree at a fairly young age—just twenty-five when he passed the bar—thirty-two when he became a judge."

She steepled her fingers and rested the tips of her forefingers on her wrinkled chin.

"So when he lost his wife to a brain tumor and his son to pneumonia, he also lost his mind trying to figure out why. His wife Deena was pregnant when she was diagnosed, and she chose to bring the baby to term instead of letting them do the experimental surgery that might have saved her life. Less than a year later, Gus' son was also gone."

She paused to let her words sink in.

"As you can imagine, it changed his world. He drank and lost his job—or rather he chose to walk away. He lost his home to financial woes along with any desire to live the privileged life he'd been living. I think he traveled to Mexico and South America and maybe other places for a while, looking for answers."

Danny was amazed that as she told Gus' tale, she didn't frown or scowl or shed a tear. He guessed she'd had many years to accept what happened to her brother. But he had to ask one thing:

"Your family didn't try to help him? Get him to come home?"

He wished immediately he hadn't said it. Sister Rose dropped her hands to her side and her mouth came open. She didn't say anything for a moment, but she appeared ready to chastise him. If Mark remembered correctly from those days so long ago, she was as good at chastising as she was at patience. Patience must have won out now, however, because her mouth slammed shut, and she sighed deeply. Her voice was soft as she continued.

"Gus and I had no one but each other by then. Our parents disowned him when he started drinking—then they both passed on. I did what I could—tried to be there for him, but Deena's death hit me pretty hard, too. I had begun my journey into the sisterhood when all this was happening and when I lost Deena to cancer, my nephew to illness, my parents to old age and Gus to his grief, I concentrated on my studies."

Casey's voice drew both Danny and Sister Rose's attention to her face.

"And obviously you kept in touch if he knew where to find you when he needed to drop Danny off for that week."

"Yes," the nun said, her voice still soft. Her shoulders sagged, and she dropped her gaze to study her own hands now resting calmly in her lap. "He wrote once or twice a year, and he visited a bit over the years. Enough for me to know he was okay." She looked up at Danny. "I didn't know he was on the streets until he showed up that day with you. I didn't find out about his death until weeks after it happened, when the police tracked me down."

They were all quiet then, the weight of what happened so many years ago suspended in the air.

After several minutes, Sister Rose finally broke the silence.

"I truly believe God looked out for him, and that he led you, Danny, to Gus's side. I guess you became the son Gus never got to raise."

Danny chewed on a forefinger thinking about it all. His chin bobbed gently as he, too, accepted that Gus was who Gus was supposed to be. He reached for Casey's hand and began gently stroking it with his thumb.

"I never would have found you, darling, if fate hadn't interceded to bring us together," he said. "I let us happen, and I'll never regret it."

"But Gus is largely responsible as well. He taught me how to take whatever happened to me and do something with it. He kept me educated by taking me to libraries. He kept me safe by teaching me when to run and when to fight. He showed me when to let go of my anger at what life dealt and learn how to accept help."

Danny pulled on his wife's hand and leaned in to plant a kiss on her forehead.

"He taught me how to become my own architect of fate."

About the Authors

F. Sharon Swope, a newspaper columnist for many years, brought her four children up to be lovers of the imagination and the written word. Spurred by the success of one of her daughters, children's book author Allyn M. Stotz, Sharon decided in her eighties that if she was ever going to write the many stories that had been bouncing around in her mind, she better get started. She sat down and created The Fate Series, which is co-authored by her other daughter Genilee Swope Parente. She and Genilee also wrote *Holiday Connections*, a collection of short stories based on U.S. holidays. Sharon has been published in several magazines. In November 2017, she turned ninety.

She lives in Woodbridge, VA.

Genilee Swope Parente makes her living as a freelance editorial consultant. She's managing editor of several magazines and newsletters, and writes and edits features articles, blogs, marketing materials, newsletter articles and more for her clients. Genilee graduated from Ohio State University with a journalism degree and was a reporter, a communications manager, a public information officer and a trade magazine editor before striking out on her own. In addition to The Fate Series, she is working on several novels of her own.

She lives in Dumfries, VA with her husband, her daughter, two dogs and a cat.

Books by F. Sharon Swope
and Genilee Swope Parente:

Twist of Fate
Wretched Fate
Violet Fate
Treasured Fate
Architect of Fate
Holiday Connections

Please visit the authors at

www.swopeparente.com
www.facebook.com/genileesharon.swopeparente
     @GenileeParente

And write them at swopeparente@gmail.com

www.ingramcontent.com/pod-product-compliance
Lightning Source LLC
Chambersburg PA
CBHW072205130726
47910CB00011B/1894